I0761971

his other lie

(a stella fall psychological suspense thriller—book 2)

ava strong

Ava Strong

Debut author Ava Strong is author of the REMI LAURENT mystery series, comprising three books (and counting); of the ILSE BECK mystery series, comprising four books (and counting); and of the STELLA FALL psychological suspense thriller series, comprising three books (and counting).

An avid reader and lifelong fan of the mystery and thriller genres, Ava loves to hear from you, so please feel free to visit www.avastrongauthor.com to learn more and stay in touch.

ISBN: 978-1-0943-9266-0

BOOKS BY AVA STRONG

REMI LAURENT FBI SUSPENSE THRILLER
THE DEATH CODE (Book #1)
THE MURDER CODE (Book #2)
THE MALICE CODE (Book #3)

ILSE BECK FBI SUSPENSE THRILLER
NOT LIKE US (Book #1)
NOT LIKE HE SEEMED (Book #2)
NOT LIKE YESTERDAY (Book #3)
NOT LIKE THIS (Book #4)

STELLA FALL PSYCHOLOGICAL SUSPENSE THRILLER
HIS OTHER WIFE (Book #1)
HIS OTHER LIE (Book #2)
HIS OTHER SECRET (Book #3)

CHAPTER ONE

Stella Fall's hand shook as she raised the gun. Its grip felt unfamiliar in her palm. The head-and-torso target, ten long yards away in the indoor shooting range, seemed like an impossible goal as she stared at it, narrowing her ice-blue eyes.

Crippling fear flooded her at what she was about to do. Joining the FBI Academy's trainee agent program had been a crazy decision. This was her first firearms training session since she'd arrived at Quantico two days ago. It felt way beyond her scope of expertise and it always would be. She didn't like guns and was scared of them. They brought back memories that she didn't want to relive. At that moment, her mother's mocking voice resounded in her mind.

"You're never going to amount to anything. You never learn. You're like your father, and look what happened to him."

She remembered her dad coming home from work, taking off his jacket and laying down his gun belt with a tired sigh before locking the weapon away. When her mother started one of their inevitable screaming fights later in the night, Stella would curl up in bed, squeezing her eyes shut, praying that Rhonda Fall never found the key to that cupboard.

Had her dad turned his trusty service pistol onto himself in the end? Had he driven somewhere he knew he'd never be found, and killed himself? Was that why he'd disappeared?

That was Stella's worst fear, the one that caused terrible nightmares, and it was why she'd never been interested in guns. Most probably, it was the reason that she'd been so strongly drawn to the field of psychology, where words could influence an outcome, rather than relying on a speeding chunk of lead.

She sensed Carrie's gaze on her and heard the tall trainee agent give a mocking laugh. Carrie was part of the new intake, and had arrived at the academy at the same time as Stella. When Stella had stepped into the dormitory with her bags, Carrie had been sitting in the small lounge, chatting with three of the men.

"I guess you guys will have to put up with having a girl in your class," she'd been joking in a confident voice as Stella passed the door.

Then Carrie had glanced sideways and, seeing Stella, her eyes had narrowed.

"Two girls, maybe?" one of the men had asked, in equally joking tones.

"Well!" Carrie had exclaimed, sounding as if her sense of humor had completely disappeared.

She'd assumed she was the only woman in the new intake, Stella realized. Instead of regarding Stella as an ally, she perceived her as a threat.

Now, Carrie had just finished her first target practice session. She was familiar with guns, as were the four other male students in the small shooting class. Stella was the only one who'd never handled them before and she'd fallen behind the others as she'd fumbled her way through the unfamiliar processes of loading, unloading, holstering, and unholstering. Everyone else was done and watching her, which only added to the unwanted pressure.

"Any time, Fall," Marc, the instructor, said loudly, sounding impatient. "It doesn't matter about accuracy the first time. Just remember what you've been taught and go through the process. Your aim and muscle memory will build."

Through her earmuffs she could hear more sniggers from Carrie and one of the men. They were laughing at her, not with her. She hadn't thought her first few days here would be anything like this.

She took a deep breath and gathered her fragmented thoughts. Dragged her mind away from her fears and instead, remembered her father's steady and pragmatic approach. There was nothing special about a gun, he'd always said. It was simply one of the tools of the trade. Never a first resort, but preferably also not a last resort. Just something to be used if necessary, in a dangerous situation.

She breathed out. Her hands had steadied and now felt rock-still. Surprisingly, she felt a competent calmness fill her.

Remembering the steps she had to take, she sighted, identified the target, and then gently squeezed the trigger.

Through her earmuffs the explosion of sound was muted. She sighted, squeezed again. Calm and sure. Center mass—the chest. Then a shot to the head. Then center mass again. Then one more to the head. And then repeat once more.

She was breathing hard as she lowered the gun, brushing away a strand of long, dark hair that had escaped from her ponytail.

Looking at the target more closely, she stared at it in surprise.

Six pretty accurate shots. The first head shot had been a couple of inches wide. The others were all on target.

"Are you sure you haven't shot before?" Marc asked, sounding incredulous. The surprise in his voice made her feel proud, but she was getting resentful looks from the men in the group, especially those who had missed shots in their first round.

Stella shook her head. "Never. My dad was a champion, though. He used to win gold in the local competitions whenever he entered."

"You've clearly inherited that ability. That's an impressive first effort. In fact, I've never seen a novice student shoot so well. You might not like guns. I see that and I understand. But when you need to use one, calmness and accuracy can save your life."

"Thank you," Stella said, glowing at the praise. She turned and smiled at Carrie, hoping that her newfound competency would help her get on friendly footing with the slim brunette, but Carrie looked furious.

Stella realized that she'd shown Carrie up by shooting better. Instead of winning her friendship, she'd now become an actual enemy.

"Let's head outside. It's time for the obstacle course training," Marc said.

They followed the stocky, muscular trainer out of the indoor range and into the sunny afternoon. It was the beginning of June and the air was fresh with recent rain, and warm with the promise of summer.

Walking at the back of the group, Stella followed the others across the well-trimmed grass and onto a gravel path which led to a wooded area. There, they met up with another group that must have finished up at one of the other shooting ranges.

As the trainees jogged on the spot, or did a few push-ups to warm up, Stella realized how fit and strong all of them looked. She wished she'd spent more time pushing weights in the gym. Running—her chosen sport—couldn't develop the strength and power she saw here.

Carrie took off her blue sweater, and Stella noticed the play of muscles in her upper arms. Everyone had been building themselves up in anticipation of coming here.

Everyone except her, thanks to her last-minute acceptance in this challenging four-month program. She hadn't had time to prepare.

"Along this path is an obstacle course. There are twenty obstacles over the distance of about a mile," Marc told them. "The obstacles will test your strength, agility, coordination, and speed. Strength is the biggest factor and the one that most new agents need to develop.

Physical injury is the most common reason for a trainee not completing the program. That's why we have gyms onsite that you are encouraged to use anytime."

Carrie nodded eagerly. Stella felt filled with doubt all over again as Marc continued.

"Being an FBI agent means being physically and mentally skilled. We need your minds, we need your relevant qualifications, you are all highly intelligent individuals. But you also need to be able to chase down and tackle a violent suspect, and defend yourself from physical attacks. So although your brains got you here, your strength and fitness will keep you here. This time around, we're including this obstacle course as part of your first physical test. In order to graduate, you have to pass at least two of the three tests. The first is now, the second midway through the course, and the final one is in the last week of your training."

Stella swallowed down her nerves. If she didn't pass, her future here would already be at stake.

"We'll send you off in pairs, so get in line. The obstacles on the left and right side of the track are identical, so it doesn't matter which you choose." Marc checked his stopwatch.

Stella shuffled into line, finding herself all the way at the back. Thankfully, Carrie was just in front of her in the same line. Stella had already pegged her as being fiercely competitive, and had worried that she might position herself as Stella's partner, looking to beat her in the obstacles to make up for the shooting range.

"First pair, go!" Marc called loudly.

Stella craned around. The path curved left, so the only obstacle she could see was a wooden ladder. She saw the first trainees, both men, scramble up the tall ladders, over the top, and down again. They did it surprisingly fast, and then they disappeared from sight.

"Next pair."

Stella felt her butterflies gather as the pairs were counted down. In front of her, Carrie was springing from foot to foot and swinging her arms, warming herself up for the challenge.

"Next pair!" Marc's shouted words broke the silence. This time it was Carrie's turn. She and her partner sped off, leaving Stella the last in her row. She watched as Carrie lithely clambered the ladder, vaulting neatly over the top rung and shimmying down again.

"Last pair!"

She was off, sprinting toward the ladder. The wooden rungs felt cold and slippery in her nervous grip. She headed up as fast as she could. Too fast, in fact. Her foot slid off the rung and she scrabbled for purchase, feeling terrified that she'd fall all the way back down while Marc was watching.

She didn't. She regained her footing and reached the top. It felt dizzyingly high and her arms were already aching. Clumsily, she scrambled over the top and down, praying she wouldn't slip again.

Pounding around the corner, she realized she was already behind the blond man who had set off at the same time as her. That meant she would be the last to return. Oh well, it was better than the humiliation of being overtaken, Stella thought, staring at the next obstacle, a high net hung between two sturdy wooden poles. It sagged and swayed as she clutched at the rough rope, hauling herself to the top and scrambling over the scarily unstable structure.

Dashing around the next bend as fast as she could, Stella negotiated a trio of wide ditches, followed by a knotted rope that had to be climbed as far as the red banner flying high above.

Seeing her arms were close to quitting on her, she used her legs to fight the battle, bracing her feet against the knots, frustrated by how the swinging of the rope resisted her attempts to get purchase.

Then, around the next bend, her worst nightmare. A row of rings hung from a beam high overhead. There was extra incentive to negotiate the line successfully because the beam was positioned over a deep, muddy ditch.

Gritting her teeth, Stella leaped for the first ring, clutching it with both hands, her arms searing with the effort. She swung back and forth gaining momentum, and then dared to let go with one hand, making a desperate grab for the next ring.

She got it. Hanging on hard, Stella repeated the process. Once more, she was successful, and from the third ring she battled her way to the fourth.

But, as she prepared to tackle the fifth ring, she realized something terrible.

The sixth ring—second last in the line—was not accessible. It was looped up, over the beam. And it wasn't humanly possible to get from ring five to seven without dropping down into the ditch.

Oh no, Stella thought. What a disaster. How had the others coped with it? Since none of them had been back by the time she left, she didn't know. Probably they'd all dropped down into the ditch, but not all of them were as far behind the time as Stella was.

She guessed she'd learn where the launderette was quicker than she'd thought. Bracing herself for the horrible tumble down, Stella let go and plummeted, sprawling into the muddy ditch. Grime coated her arms and legs, spattered her face. It took forever to scramble up its slippery sides.

When she arrived back, there was a burst of derogatory sniggers from the sweaty and grimy team waiting by the finish.

Stella expected that they would also have been covered in mud. But none of them were. How had they avoided having to let go? she wondered, feeling unfairly singled out.

"Had some trouble with the rings?" Marc asked. "You've gone over time, I'm afraid. Ten seconds too slow. That's a fail. Everyone else, you got a pass."

"There was a problem with the rings," Stella said, wanting to explain.

"Yes, we can see that, Fall," Marc quipped, and all the others burst into louder laughter.

Stella noticed Carrie's triumphant grin. She was howling with laughter, clutching at her flat, taut stomach.

Only then did it hit her.

Carrie had sabotaged the course. Stella had gone after her, the final one to do that left-hand route. Carrie must have hung onto the last ring, turned back, and thrown the previous one up over the top pole, knowing that Stella wouldn't make it.

How could anyone do such a thing? Stella couldn't believe the vindictiveness of the action. And the sabotage had succeeded beyond Carrie's wildest dreams, as it had taken up those few precious seconds that had made the difference between a pass and a fail.

Her future here was in jeopardy. One more fail and she'd be thrown out.

Perhaps she'd end up not making the cut in any case. All her fears surged back. She was hopeless, hated by the others, and would never be good enough.

But though she felt completely demoralized, in that moment she found a fire inside her, an inner strength she hadn't known she possessed.

So what if she was slow and had embarrassed herself in front of all her fellow trainees? She could strengthen and spend time in the gym.

And so what if the others were going to give her a hard time? She wasn't here to make friends, and in any case the best way to win friendship would be to show she was worthy of respect and had the guts to try again.

You can do this, she told herself, as she turned her back on Carrie's mocking gaze and strode away, brushing mud off her arms. Stick it out. Even if you feel like this again, you can always come back fighting. You're going to graduate, Stella Fall, and more importantly, you're going to do it at the top of your class.

CHAPTER TWO

Four months later.

Cara Garcia hurried along the road. She'd gotten off a stop too early by mistake, as the last time when she'd come for her interview, she'd traveled from the agency office. That was in Fairfield, one of the prettiest towns Cara had ever seen. She loved the characterful New England architecture, the steep roofs and massive chimneys a reflection of the area's colonial history. She appreciated the colorful store and restaurant frontages, and how neat and clean it was. And such beautiful trees, adorned in their rich, fall colors.

This time, she'd traveled from her apartment, which was an hour's journey away and in a very different area. Definitely, the last ten minutes were the most pleasant part of the trip, as the walk took her along a road bordering the sea. Glancing at the golden beach and azure waves, with the breeze cool on her face, Cara felt hopeful that her new job would start out well.

Fairfield was a prestigious area to work, and her new employers were wealthy people. This was her chance to better herself in a higher-paying job, even though the traveling time was long and the job itself might well be demanding.

The husband, Mr. Logan, had been a friendly person. She'd liked him immediately during the quick interview last week. He'd seemed kind and fair. But she had yet to meet his wife, and this would be her biggest challenge. If his wife got along with her, all would be well during her two-week trial. If the wife didn't like her, then the trial would not be successful and she might not work in this big, beautiful house for long.

With a pang of nerves, Cara hoped that she would get along with her. She'd heard scary stories from her friends about what could happen if a new maid clashed with the wife. One person she knew had been fired on the very first day after making a minor mistake.

She turned inland, heading down the curving road, checking her watch again. She was supposed to start at seven-thirty and already it was twenty past. She broke into a jog, checking the map on her phone as she reached the corner ahead.

Here was the house, third from the corner, opposite a park.

Mr. Logan had given his instructions with a smile. “Knock on the door and introduce yourself to my wife. She’ll show you what to do and give you a key to let yourself in next time.”

Breathless, Cara arrived on the doorstep, taking a moment to straighten her hair and tug her blouse straight. First impressions counted. She really wanted Mrs. Logan to like her. This was a desperately important moment.

She lifted the brass knocker, tapped three times, and waited, listening.

There was no answer from inside and Cara felt her stomach twist. Already, things weren’t going as planned. Why?

Checking her watch, she saw she was five minutes early. Perhaps Mrs. Logan wasn’t yet back from the gym or shopping. Although she assumed it would be locked, she tried the door. To her surprise it swung smoothly open. She was confronted again by the large, majestic house, smelling faintly of fresh paint, its wooden floors gleaming, and its furniture brand new and sparkling clean.

“Good morning?” she called.

Goose bumps prickled on her arms. There was a weird feel about this place. The silence felt oppressive. Why had that door been open when there wasn’t a soul around? Surely if you were upstairs in the bedroom or the bathroom, you would lock the front door?

Had Mrs. Logan stepped out quickly? Maybe she’d gone next door, or into the garden? She waited another minute but the silence continued and she had no idea what to do.

Cara had been inside houses before after robberies had taken place and crimes had occurred. This house gave her that same prickling sensation, even though nothing looked out of place.

Or was there?

Yes, there was. She could see it now.

Her gaze was drawn to one of the pictures on the wall by the foot of the stairs. It was knocked askew as if someone had brushed past it while on the way down. Or perhaps on the way up, Cara thought uneasily.

She should check nothing was wrong.

“Mrs. Logan?” she called loudly.

Nobody could have gone past that picture without straightening it. Nobody! Why was it like that?

Her heart now pounding with worry, Cara stepped inside, closing the door behind her. She put her purse down under the hall table and then headed to the stairs. Reaching the picture—a framed line drawing of a tree—she straightened it carefully.

She hadn't been up the stairs before. As she walked up, she felt like a trespasser, someone who was prying into private space without permission. At the top, she hesitated again and looked around. There were closed doors to the left and right, but she guessed from her previous experience in a similar home that the master bedroom would be the one straight ahead, at the end of the corridor. That door was ajar.

Something didn't smell right up here. The fresh aromas she had picked up downstairs were overshadowed by something else, a subtle yet unpleasant tinge in the air.

"Good morning," she called in the most cheerful tone she could summon up, as she approached the door. By now, all her instincts were screaming at her, but still she was hoping that by some miracle it might all be okay, that Mrs. Logan had been in the bathroom and would greet her warmly.

No response. Just more of the echoing silence. And as she reached the door, the smell was stronger—a thick, metallic odor.

Feeling desperately worried now, Cara gathered her courage and pushed the door wide.

And, as the bloody scene inside imprinted itself on her appalled gaze, she screamed at the top of her voice, yelling out again and again in terror and shock.

"No! It can't be! Mr. Logan! Your wife! Your wife is dead!"

CHAPTER THREE

Heading outside to the obstacle course, Stella couldn't believe how far she had come in a short time. Four months after her arrival at Quantico as a new trainee agent, she'd changed, and so had her surroundings. When she'd arrived, the view had been early summer green. Now, it was the beginning of October. Some trees were red and gold, others were bare, and the sky was cloudy and gray.

She'd just completed the last written tests in her syllabus, and yesterday, she and her team had all passed the infamous "pepper spray" exam. Her eyes still stung from the memory of being pepper sprayed in the face, and then having to force her streaming eyes open and defend herself against the instructor trying to grab her pistol out of its holster.

Now, surveying the final course route, Stella only felt calm confidence. Her arms were strong, still lean but with a wiry power that allowed her to chin the bar easily ten times. Even twenty.

She was sure she'd beat her time on the suspended rings, and the trio of high nets, and the wobbly log. And the timed sprint, from one white-painted branch to another a hundred yards away.

Or was she? Was there anything that could go wrong?

With a sudden premonition, Stella bent down and double-checked her sports boots. With comfortable, grippy soles and soft leather uppers, they fit her like a second skin and had lasted the whole way through her training months. Apart from one time when she'd almost lost a boot halfway through the second of her three graded physical tests. The lace on her right boot had snapped, which she'd thought was very strange because they were still new and good quality. Even so, she'd managed to complete the test with seconds to spare, and achieve a passing grade.

Now, feeling suddenly suspicious, Stella examined the laces again.

Her eyebrows shot up as she realized the lace of the left-hand boot was cut through almost to breaking point. Undoubtedly, as she'd started to run, it would have snapped.

That would have put her entire test, and her overall pass grade, in jeopardy.

With a rush of anger, Stella knew that this was Carrie's work.

She was hell bent on being the only woman to graduate from their intake. Ever since Stella's appearance in the dormitory had shattered Carrie's complacency, she'd done her best to make life hell for her. Stella had quickly realized her behavior was ego-driven. Women were much scarcer in the program, and Carrie had started out assuming she'd be the only female in her group to complete one of the most difficult training programs that law enforcement officers could go through.

It was unfortunate that Stella had proved to be not only the better shooter, but also stronger academically throughout the program. Although Stella had bonded with the other trainees over the past months, Carrie had refused to relent. Month after month, she'd seen Carrie's frustration and ultra-competitive nature boil over into acts of meanness and sabotage.

Stella had been constantly taunted by her snide comments and needling. There was the time she'd stolen Stella's notes from her bag before a criminal procedure test. And when they'd been partnered together during a bank-robbery exercise in the infamous role-playing area of the academy known as Hogan's Alley, Carrie had failed to warn Stella of an approaching criminal behind her. That had earned Stella a reprimand for carelessness, even though at the time she'd been tracking another fugitive and had asked Carrie to watch her back.

And now, there was the second shoelace incident, designed once again to make sure Stella would fail a physical test that she had to pass in order to graduate.

Controlling her anger and trying to keep calm as she assessed the problem, Stella realized she could snap the broken lace and tie a knot. It wasn't ideal but at least her boot wouldn't come off.

Quickly she completed the emergency repair.

"Shoes all good to go?" Brian, her partner, asked teasingly and Stella smiled back, feeling in a better frame of mind now this was done. The blond man who'd set off at the same time as her on the very first obstacle course, also battling with his own physical fitness, had become a friend after his initial distrust of her. She'd grown to respect him and she hoped it was mutual.

"All good now, yes," she said.

And then she heard a mocking voice from behind her. "Really? I don't think you're good. You don't look well prepared at all."

Stella spun around, her temper flaring again as she saw Carrie smiling superciliously at her. "You're going to fail," Carrie added.

Brian turned around too, looking annoyed by Carrie's words. A few others muttered in surprise at the comment. Stella felt a flash of anger.

"What do you mean by that?" she asked politely. There was a week to go until graduation! Why couldn't Carrie leave it be? Why did she continually have to fling out insults?

Their small group was now the only one left, and Stella couldn't wait for their timed rounds to start. Hopefully she could get away and start running, focusing on that, rather than on this incessant taunting.

"Well, your first time around an obstacle course didn't go very well. In fact, it proved you were the class loser," Carrie said, spreading her hands in an "aw shucks" way. "I have a feeling today will be the same for you and you might not get a passing grade. Call it instinct."

Anger blazed through Stella. Enough was enough. They were supposed to be a team. The FBI was all about teamwork. Not about causing divisions and trying to ruin others' rounds. She wasn't prepared to accept this any longer. Not for another moment.

"Unfortunately, you're out of luck. Because I noticed you cut almost all the way through my shoelace, and I fixed it. Pity I didn't pick it up last time, but at least I did this time."

Carrie was now looking absolutely furious. Letting all her resentment out, Stella continued. "And as for our first test, maybe I wouldn't have come last if the person who went before me hadn't deliberately sabotaged the course. And she never admitted to it. Not exactly in line with the FBI's principles of candor and integrity," Stella shot back.

"What?" Carrie glared at her, looking outraged. "Are you accusing me of doing that? So you're calling me a liar?"

"I'm not calling you anything," Stella said calmly. "Your actions speak louder, don't they?"

Snarling with rage, Carrie tensed, bunching her hands into fists.

In a horrified moment, Stella realized she was actually going to start a physical fight. It was forbidden at the academy, and rightly so. What Carrie was doing could get them both expelled.

There was only one way out of this. Stella had to act first. Just as she'd learned in her training, she had to actively defend herself, and neutralize the threat.

Acting as fast as she could, she did what she'd been longing to do from the time she first started at the academy, before she'd had the muscle memory or the know-how to do it effectively.

She drew her right hand back and punched Carrie as hard as she could in her solar plexus.

The breath huffed out of Carrie.

She doubled over, gasping for air, and as she did that, Stella grabbed her shoulder and kicked her legs out from under her so she sprawled on her backside on the muddy ground.

"Neutralized, I think," Stella said, sounding satisfied.

Carrie was opening and closing her mouth like a fish out of water, unable to say anything in response. How refreshing, Stella thought, allowing herself a moment to enjoy the revenge she'd finally been able to take.

Then she ran forward to take her place at the starting point.

"Next pair!" Marc's voice was loud, cutting through the tension of the moment. Stella sprinted away. Her hand was throbbing from the force of the blow, but victory gave her feet wings. Carrie had gotten what she'd deserved, what she'd been pushing for ever since she'd started her bitchiness. And now, Stella was going to kill this course.

It was only as she raced away that she realized the true idiocy of what she'd just done. Carrie had set a trap for her, and Stella, in a hotheaded moment, had walked straight in.

She'd acted in self-defense before Carrie had even raised her arms, and that meant Carrie could claim Stella had assaulted her. Deliberate assault of a fellow trainee was an even more serious offense than a physical fight, and could undoubtedly get her expelled from the academy.

If Carrie chose to escalate this, and Stella knew she would, then her entire career would be at stake.

CHAPTER FOUR

Breathless and spent, Stella used the last remaining strength in her legs to power over the finish line, before staggering to a tree. She leaned against it, her arms quivering, gasping for breath.

In another minute, Carrie would cross the line. When she did, Stella decided she was going to walk straight over to her and apologize. Despite having been baited by the tall brunette, the punch had been unacceptable. Her superiors would believe it showed a loss of control, even though she'd felt fully in control and as if it had been the only sensible course of action to defuse a potential attack.

Gulping in oxygen, Stella was planning her apology, when there was a tap on her shoulder.

She straightened up, releasing her grip on the rough bark, feeling a twinge of guilt that Marc had seen what happened.

It wasn't Marc. The person standing there, regarding her with a hard expression, was Thom, one of the academy's most senior instructors.

Stella's heart sank.

"Sir," she greeted him, trying not to sound breathless or worried, and aware she was probably failing on both counts.

"Ms. Fall. You're wanted in the director's office. Now."

This was it. Someone had seen what she did and reported her. She'd messed up badly and now she would suffer the full consequences of her stupid, reckless actions.

Filled with panic, Stella wondered if she should stammer out an apology there and then but decided against it. That wasn't how the FBI worked. There were no last-minute excuses, and no second chances for seriously bad decisions. She'd made her choice and now she would have to bear the consequences of whatever came her way.

She realized that mud-streaked and sweaty, she looked a fright.

"Do you mean immediately, sir?" she asked. "Or may I change clothes first?"

"You must change clothes, but do it quickly," Thom warned.

This was worse than bad. Her idiocy had put everything at risk. All the months of training had been for nothing.

She rushed back to the dormitories, which at this hour of the day were all empty. Quickly, shaking with nerves, she showered and brushed her hair and changed into a fresh pair of pants and a clean T-shirt. As an afterthought she grabbed her smart FBI jacket. If she was being told to change, it might be that she was going to be kicked out immediately. At least she'd have something warm to wear.

She felt a sense of doom as she went into the building and followed the route that led to the director's offices, preparing herself to take her punishment on the chin, knowing that this might be the last time she walked down this glass-lined corridor.

She headed up to the wooden door on leaden feet.

The door was ajar. Stella tapped, waited, and then pushed it open and walked into the small reception room. Its furniture was highly polished, and the walls were lined with framed photographs and memorabilia, as well as some official notices.

The room was empty, which she hadn't expected. This was where the director's assistant usually worked, but he wasn't sitting behind the desk. Instead, she heard voices from the main office beyond.

They must be in there, discussing her fate.

Should she wait here, or knock on the inner office door? Trainees didn't usually go into that sacrosanct space, but were dealt with in the reception room. She hesitated, feeling nervousness fill her, not knowing which choice would be correct.

As she hesitated, the voices behind the far door grew louder and then it opened.

"Thanks! See you soon," a cheerful voice called out.

Stella had expected the assistant to walk out, but to her shock, she saw someone she never expected to be here. Turning toward her, his face breaking into a grin as he saw her, was Clem.

Her mouth dropped open in surprise. What on earth was he doing here?

Clem had been Stella's mentor during her studies at the University of Chicago, and had become a good friend. The tall, rangy, gray-haired man, who had retired ten years ago after a brilliant career as an FBI special agent and criminal profiler, was the one who'd put in a good word for her, shared her master's thesis on serial killer mentality, and gotten her accepted into the academy.

Had he called her here? Stella's mind spun with confusion.

Clem strode toward her, gripping her hand in a firm greeting.

“Stella. Good to see you. I hear you’ve excelled. You’re in the top five percent academically, and the top twenty-five percent physically. Your shooting ability is exceptional. Congratulations.”

Stella blinked. “Thank you,” she said, finding her manners after an astounded pause. Clem hadn’t come here just to praise her for her grades. What was this all about, and why was she not going straight into a disciplinary hearing?

“Come with me.”

“Come with you? Where?”

As confused as she was, this didn’t sound as if she was about to be expelled. So there must be something else afoot.

“I need your help,” he said, sounding as serious as she’d ever heard him.

“I—sure. How can I help?” Stella asked, not knowing what to say.

“Follow me. We’re heading off campus.”

Clem turned and walked briskly to the building’s exit door, but didn’t head toward the parking lot as she’d expected. Instead, he took the path leading to the helipad.

“Where are we going? Are we flying somewhere?” she asked, just to confirm that this was really happening.

“We’re going to the FBI field office in New Haven.” Clem sounded calmly satisfied. “I was there earlier this morning. One of the pilots was heading here to transport an instructor so I called in a favor and hitched a ride.”

“The FBI office?” Stella repeated, just to check she’d gotten the facts right and this wasn’t some kind of complicated dream.

Clem nodded mysteriously.

Stella climbed into the helicopter with a breathless “Good morning” to the pilot. She took the earphones handed to her, put them on, sat in one of the back seats, and fastened her belt.

The radio crackled, and in another minute they were taking off, the ground falling away from them as they lifted into the cloudy air.

Despite the numbers of helicopters at the academy, Stella had only ridden in them twice for basic training exercises. She’d never been on a trip outside the borders of the larger Marine Corps training grounds where the academy was situated. She stared out the window, fascinated by the scenery passing by as the copter banked and headed north.

With the headphones and the noise, there was no opportunity for any conversation and that meant that during the hour-long ride there was nothing for her to do except try to figure out what was happening.

She came up blank. She couldn't see a reason for any of this to be happening, and wished she had some clues that she could use to prepare.

What on earth was Clem getting her involved in?

*

By the time they landed at the New Haven field office, the clouds had cleared and the morning was mild with autumnal sunshine.

Clem climbed out and Stella followed him, hurrying from the helipad toward the main office. She'd never been here, never even seen a picture of it, and was surprised by its size and scale. She and Clem headed up the stairs to the main entrance of this massive brick building. With its tinted windows, it looked at once utilitarian and intimidating.

She'd never thought she'd be back in Connecticut again so soon. She'd moved to Greenwich when she'd been engaged, but her nightmare stay there had been cut short when her fiancé was murdered. Having finally managed to clear her name and escape his toxic family, who were now suffering legal consequences for their own misdoings, Stella had been glad to leave and had no desire to return.

After going through security Clem headed purposefully down one of the corridors, checking the time on his watch as he strode along.

Outside one of the doors he stopped and turned to her.

"You good?" he asked. His tone was calm, as always, but his eyes carried a hint of concern for her.

"Yes. I'm good," she said, hoping he couldn't tell how nervous she was feeling.

He nodded, looking satisfied. Then he tapped on the door.

It was opened almost immediately by a harassed-looking man who looked to be in his late forties. His chestnut-brown hair was a couple of weeks overdue for a cut, and his hazel eyes narrowed when they saw Stella. Immediately, she sensed his animosity.

"You're Stella Fall?" he asked sharply, confirming Stella's initial suspicion that for him, she wasn't welcome.

"I am, sir," she replied, trying to sound confident, which she wasn't, rather than confused and intimidated, which she was.

"Stella is in her final week at the academy. She's due to graduate next week," Clem said. "Stella, this is Adrian Roth. He's an FBI supervisory special agent."

A special agent? Stella drew in a quick breath.

"It's good to meet you," she said, feeling awestruck.

Roth sighed, looking frustrated.

"Come into my office," he said to Clem. Stella was clearly not included in the invitation. The door closed firmly behind the men, leaving her outside.

She could hear muttered voices. Then Roth's rose angrily.

"She's a trainee! She hasn't even graduated yet!"

Would she ever graduate? Fear clenched Stella's gut as she remembered that moment of lost control. She'd attacked Carrie in front of their entire training group! What had she been thinking?

More low voices followed. Roth didn't want her here, that was obvious from his body language and the words she'd overheard. Would Clem be successful? What would the outcome be?

Then the door was flung open and she jumped.

Roth strode out, followed by Clem. Clem glanced at her and his lips twitched. Stella thought he was suppressing a smug smile.

"Stella, Roth and I have discussed your involvement in a new case that closely fits your experience. I happened to be here in New Haven when it was called in. I suggested that even though you have not yet graduated, the team should bring you on board, as your insight will be valuable," Clem explained. "After some discussion, we've agreed that you will participate."

It had sounded more like a serious argument, but anyway. That aside, how could they possibly need her insight? What kind of case was this?

Thinking of her own recent experiences, Stella felt a flash of fear. She swallowed it down, replying in a calm tone, "I'll gladly help in any way I can."

Roth's lips tightened. "This is extremely unorthodox," he shot back.

It was very clear that there hadn't yet been any real agreement and that Clem had either persuaded, or somehow overridden, the supervisory special agent.

Clem nodded calmly. "It is unorthodox, I agree. But since Stella is so close to graduating, the academy director himself gave permission for her to be involved."

So Clem had gone over Roth's head. No wonder resentment radiated from him.

If the director had heard what she'd done earlier today and that she would be facing a disciplinary hearing on her return, there was no way he'd have allowed it. Now, she feared that her wrongdoings would catch up with her at any moment. She hoped she'd manage to offer some value on this case before they did.

Roth shrugged. "It's highly irregular for a trainee agent to get involved, even though you say she has unique insights, and that her experience and perception will help us."

Stella swallowed. It sounded like Clem had talked her up big-time. She already had massive expectations to live up to, and she didn't even know what this was about.

"You are here in a job shadowing capacity only," Roth said warningly, turning to Stella. "We are investigating a serious crime which is potentially the work of a serial killer. We can't allow trainees to run wild on the scene. You'll do what I say, go where I tell you, keep your mouth shut and your eyes open. Unless you have something of real value to add, bottom line is—you stay out of our way."

"I will, sir," Stella consented humbly. Her heart was pounding with excitement and nerves. "I hope I can add value to the investigation. And I promise you, even though I'm not experienced, I'll do my best, as I have always done ever since I signed up for my training. If you include me in your team, I will make sure I earn my place on it."

It seemed like standing up for her strengths this way was the right decision. Her confident words mollified Roth, and his angry expression softened.

"I hope you will be an asset," he agreed. "But don't call me sir. I'm not an academy instructor. You can call me Roth."

"Glad everything's sorted," Clem confirmed, sounding happy that they'd reached an agreement. "I'll leave you to it, then. Good luck. I'll be in touch."

Stella stared in alarm as he turned and strode away. She'd expected him to stay, at least for a while. She couldn't help feeling he'd thrown her to the wolves.

"We must head to the scene right away," Roth said.

This would be her first crime scene. Well, her first real one. She'd completed projects during her academy training. Even though the instructors had thrown every challenge and obstacle they could into the students' path, she knew there would be many more unforeseen hurdles coming her way in real life.

"Maxwell," Roth snapped out as he passed the adjoining office.

A fit-looking man in his twenties, with buzz-cut dark hair and sunglasses pushed up onto his head, rushed out. He hesitated when he saw Stella, looking at her in astonishment.

Seeing Roth was striding ahead and not offering any introductions, Stella took the opportunity.

"Hi. I'm Stella Fall," she said.

Hustling along beside her, Maxwell frowned.

"You're the academy graduate?" He didn't sound pleased.

"Not yet. I'm about a week away from graduating," Stella said, her stomach knotting again as she remembered she was actually about a day away from a disciplinary hearing. "You are?" she asked.

"Rick Maxwell. I didn't think you were going to be here. Roth said absolutely no when Clem suggested you." Maxwell sounded like he approved of Roth's decision. "I guess he went over Roth's head."

Did nobody except Clem want her here?

Stella shrugged. "I don't know who okayed it, but Clem thought I might provide some insights on the case."

"Do you know what the case is?" Maxwell asked.

Stella had to confess her ignorance.

"Not yet," she said.

Maxwell's exasperated sigh said it all. He marched ahead of her and to her surprise, she heard him mutter something about "spoiled privileged kids with connections."

Was he talking about her? How could he possibly have gotten such a wrong impression?

Feeling even more confused, and at a serious disadvantage, Stella scrambled into the back of the silver Ford in the parking lot, as the two men opened the front doors.

"Can you tell me more about the case?" Stella asked the back of Roth's head, as he pulled out of the parking lot. She wasn't going to ask Maxwell, who clearly didn't want to speak to her and was in a sulk over her mere presence.

Luckily Roth's mood had improved slightly now that he was behind the wheel.

"It's a stabbing," he said. "A Fairfield resident was stabbed to death last night in her own bedroom."

Stella caught her breath. She stared ahead, memories flooding back, feeling suddenly sick as Roth swung the car around a corner.

A stabbing in a bedroom. That was exactly how Vaughn Marshall, her late fiancé, had died. No wonder Clem had wanted her involved. The problem was that Stella didn't know if she was ready for this. She'd suppressed the horrific memories, seeing his sightless eyes, the bloodstains rusty dark on the white sheets, the smears on her own skin that still gave her screaming nightmares.

She didn't know if she could face another scene like that. What would happen when she walked into that room, when already she felt as if she was heading to catastrophe?

Which would be more career-limiting? she wondered in a panic, as her stomach churned with sudden and violent nausea. Throwing up in Roth's unmarked, or asking him to pull over so she could vomit on the side of the road?

One of the two would happen any moment. She was sure of it.

CHAPTER FIVE

Stella buzzed the window down, letting a blast of cold wind into the car. Gulping the chilly air deeply, wiping perspiration from her forehead, she battled down her sickness. Every gasp represented a small victory as the nausea slowly subsided.

Maxwell turned, looking annoyed.

"Is there a reason we're suddenly riding in a fridge?" he asked irritably.

"Sorry." Stella buzzed it closed again, glad that her involuntary reaction to these memories had now passed. "Why is the FBI involved in the case?" she asked, hearing the wobble in her own voice but trying to keep calm.

Roth replied. "We were called in because of the possible serial aspect. Two nights ago, another woman was stabbed to death in her home in Waterbury. That's about twenty-five miles away so this may be the work of an area-specific killer. We'll have to look for any link or similarity in the circumstances during the investigation."

Stella's mouth felt dry. "What are the circumstances in this case?" she asked. Her throat was dry, too, and her voice came out hoarse. She cleared her throat, shoving her hands under her legs because she knew they were shaking.

"The victim recently moved to the Gold Coast. Relocated with her husband. He was hired as CFO for a tech company with headquarters in Fairfield. They've been here a couple of months."

"Obviously earning well, to live where they do," Maxwell added.

"Yes. He's a high earner, and hard worker, too. He was at work on the night she was killed—apparently. Being relatively new in town, they didn't know anyone well. Neither of them have a criminal record, or any history of violence. So we have no solid leads for the case, which is another reason to look out for a serial aspect."

"What's her name?" Stella asked.

"Her name?" Roth sounded surprised.

"The victim's name. I just wondered." Stella felt instinctively that knowing her name would somehow help define her as a person.

"Amanda Logan," Roth said.

He sounded as if he was slipping back into his grumpy mood. As he left the highway and wound his way into exclusive-looking suburbia, Stella thought about what he'd said. There were disturbing similarities to her recent ordeal. There had been no immediately obvious suspects when Vaughn had been murdered—apart from herself. She'd been forced into investigating to clear her name, and had ended up solving the crime.

She'd done that by digging into the backgrounds and relationships. Investigating everyone who could possibly have been involved. Asking questions, which hadn't been easy since people were suspicious and resentful of her.

She guessed that would be the only course of action here, too. At any rate, remembering what she'd done, and having the basics of a plan in place, made her feel less fearful of approaching the scene.

Amanda was a pretty name. Stella wondered how old she was. She made a guess that she would be in her late twenties or early thirties, if her husband was busy scaling a steep career ladder. It felt weird to think that she'd be closely scrutinizing the life she'd led, following in her footsteps all the way up to its shocking end.

"This is the road. Begonia Drive," Roth muttered.

The houses were big and grand with wide, green verges and exquisite front lawns. She recognized the type of area. It closely resembled Greenwich, where her ex had lived. The similarities in the cases were stacking up, she thought uneasily, wondering if this really was a serial murder or if Clem had suspected otherwise, believing the killer was part of the local community and known to the victim.

A house near the corner had several vehicles parked outside. That was the crime scene, Stella recognized with a chill.

Roth parked behind the other cars and they got out. Immediately, she heard the crackle of walkie-talkies and felt the tension in the air. She picked up a strong smell of the sea, although she couldn't see it in this well-treed suburb and had no idea which direction the beach was.

Beyond the green lawn, she saw the double-story colonial home. The walls were white-painted, and stone cladding surrounded the elegant front porch. The front door stood open and two police officers were outside. One was talking urgently on the phone. The other was taking the opportunity to smoke, dragging deeply on a cigarette as if he were racing against time.

The acrid fragrance of the smoke wafted over to Stella as she followed the other men to the door. The officer on the right ended his call and looked inquiringly at them.

"FBI," Roth said, tweaking his jacket open to show his badge. "Special Agent Roth."

The police sprang to attention. The smoker hastily stomped on his smoldering butt before respectfully picking it up again and placing it in a plastic bag.

"Morning, gents. And lady," the smoker added apologetically, noticing Stella. "Come inside. Our detectives are busy on the scene. Investigator in charge is Detective Grant. He's in the living room. Please put on gloves, head covers, and foot covers before you walk in." He indicated a box at the door.

Stella put on the protective equipment and then walked inside behind the men, her senses prickling as she took in the feel and details of this large home. She trod over gleaming hardwood floorboards. The hall was spacious and bright, with a blue-toned seascape dominating the wall above the table.

Her head snapped to the right as she picked up the sound of muffled sobs from the adjoining room. It was the living room, accessed through a large archway, and furnished in the same way—light, bright, and white. On the chaise lounge on the right, a dark-haired woman was hunched over, sobbing. A group of men were in the center of the room, standing on an enormous Persian rug. The man facing Stella, a tall man with sandy hair, looked pale and shell-shocked. He swiped a hand over his eyes and her stomach twisted in sympathy. This must be Amanda's husband.

One of the group peeled off and hurried over.

"FBI? I'm Detective Grant."

Grant was a short, balding man in a shirt and tie. His sleeves were rolled up and his features looked good-natured, although a harassed frown creased his brow.

"Special Agents Roth and Maxwell. And Stella Fall, trainee agent," Roth said.

Grant looked briefly surprised as he glanced at her.

"Shall we step out of the room?" Roth asked. Stella guessed he wanted to ask more questions out of earshot of the others.

Glancing again around the living room, Stella noticed the walls were bare. There was a surprising lack of expensive artwork although the furniture looked top-end. Had there been a robbery? Surely Roth would have said?

As they turned away and headed out, another idea occurred to her. The Logans were new money. Brand, shiny new money. So new they hadn't yet had a chance to fully deck out their enormous house with all its requisite trappings. She guessed this job had been a big step up; their ticket to a different and more luxurious lifestyle.

"We're almost finished in there," Grant explained. "We've already questioned Cara, the cleaner, who found the victim this morning, and we've done a preliminary interview with Craig, Amanda's husband, although he's still very shocked. We've told them you're involved and they need to wait here for further questioning. In the meantime, do you want to go upstairs and view the scene?" He spoke the last few words in a voice close to a whisper. Stella liked that he was clearly being considerate of the bereaved husband's feelings.

"Why didn't Craig find the victim?" she asked curiously, and then flinched inwardly as Roth swung round and glared at her. She'd forgotten all about the "keep your mouth shut" warning in her puzzlement over the logistics.

"He was pulling an all-nighter at the office. Quite common, apparently. He told us he works sixty-plus hours a week. But you can confirm those details just now," Grant said.

The wide showpiece staircase had a landing halfway up. There, an arched window looked out over a back courtyard with a modern-looking fountain streaming down over white marble, and a square of immaculate grass.

Someone must keep the yard in shape, Stella thought, wondering if Amanda had an interest in gardening, or what other staff they employed.

On the landing, Grant paused.

"Just so you know, the home didn't have any additional security installed over and above the front door locks—which show no sign of being forced, and the cleaner reported the door was unlocked when she arrived this morning."

"Why no security?" Roth asked.

"They had an appointment with a company this week to install cameras, beams, and so on. Craig said with the new job and all, there hadn't been time to do it earlier."

Stella had the sense that both Roth and Maxwell were absorbing this important information like sponges. They both nodded thoughtfully.

Then Grant continued up the staircase.

The stairs led straight into an open-plan upstairs family room. She guessed this had been designed as a children's room or game room, but the Logans didn't seem to have children and clearly hadn't known what to do with it, so it was basically an open, unfurnished space. Or not. She saw a rolled up mat in the corner, and a pair of weights. So this was where they did their yoga and weightlifting. Perhaps they'd planned to turn it into a mini gym.

Heading down the long corridor, they passed by four closed doors. The one at the end was open and Stella felt her unease deepen as she walked toward it. Her heart was pounding and her hands felt cold and wet inside the gloves. She remembered vividly the sheer terror of having woken up next to a blood-soaked corpse. Images that her subconscious had repressed were surfacing into her mind again. Vaughn's blindly staring eyes, his open mouth, that weird, porcelain-pale cast to his skin.

She breathed deeply again, glad that she would be viewing this scene on an empty stomach.

Grant led the way inside.

"The body has been removed. Otherwise, the scene is exactly as it was. Nothing's been disturbed."

Stella gulped air as she approached the room. Please, she begged herself, don't faint or collapse or do anything unprofessional because your own memories are overwhelming you.

Feeling sick with dread, she stepped inside.

CHAPTER SIX

The bloodstains caught Stella's attention immediately, huge and shocking, great crimson stains and smears on the pristine white duvet and pillows that were tangled on the king-size four-poster bed.

She stared at them, facing her fears.

Breathed in, breathed out.

To her surprise, she felt calmer now, as if the worst was over. She no longer felt that she might throw up. Instead, she felt a terrible sadness that this crime had occurred, and a steely resolve to find out who had done this act.

A beautiful woman, a pristine house with no sign of forced entry, and a shockingly violent murder.

The keys to this seemingly impossible situation had to be hidden somewhere, and she felt determined to find out what they were.

Thinking back to her own experience, she remembered that it had been the smallest details that had finally pointed the way to the killer. They could provide the most valuable clues, if she was able to notice them.

What subtle yet important details could she pick up in this scene that might lead her to the killer? Stella wondered, staring around the room.

As she surveyed the otherwise immaculate bedroom in her search for hidden clues, Stella tuned into the conversation taking place between the agents and Grant.

"What position was the victim in?" Roth asked.

"She was lying on her back on the bedcovers and was unclothed. There were multiple wounds to her chest and stomach. We've photographed the scene and the pathologist is doing the postmortem now," Grant said.

"Signs of a struggle?" Maxwell questioned.

"Yes, there is evidence that she briefly tried to defend herself. Her right palm was sliced open and you can see a couple of handprints on the bedcovers. But it was a short struggle," he concluded heavily.

"What about the time of death?" Roth said

"The initial estimate is between seven and eleven p.m. They might be able to narrow that down after the postmortem."

"Any sign of the murder weapon?"

"No, but there is a knife missing from the butcher's block in the kitchen. Mr. Logan said the set was complete the last time he looked. The measurements of the wounds and the estimated size of the missing knife seem to tally."

So most likely, the killer had used a weapon that he or she had found onsite. That was important information, Stella thought. It meant that the killer hadn't arrived armed. Had he, or she, intended to kill at all? Had there been a fight? Had Amanda surprised an intruder, or had something else gone wrong?

Of course, the killer could also have known about the knife, which again pointed to the husband as the main suspect. On the vanity in the corner, she spotted a wedding photo. Curious, she walked over to look.

Amanda had been very attractive. She smiled into the camera, blue eyes sparkling above a wide, generous mouth. Shiny auburn hair curled to her shoulders. With his arm around her, Craig looked every inch the adoring husband, and a million miles away from the wreck of a man downstairs.

She felt desperately sorry for him. At the same time, he could have committed the crime. The spouse was always a prime suspect. Sympathy must not get in the way of an impartial investigation.

Beyond the desk Stella saw a door that led to a separate dressing room, and another that led to the bathroom. Curious, wondering if there was any evidence to be found here, she stepped through.

The tub was swimming-pool size, gleaming with shine. It doubled as a shower; there was a massive rain shower head set into the ceiling above. She couldn't see so much as a droplet of water anywhere within its spotless expanse.

Only in the basin did Stella find a couple of splash marks. The basin soap was damp.

The bath towels and mat, however, lay pristine and perfectly folded on the shelf by the bath. She wasn't sure what that meant or if it meant anything at all. It was just a detail to note. Her instructors at Quantico had stressed time after time that the details could make all the difference.

Maxwell glanced at her as she came out. She thought he looked disappointed that she hadn't gone in there to faint or be sick. Fervently, she wished her senior investigators did not resent her presence here so badly.

"Shall we head downstairs?" Grant asked.

"Yes," Roth agreed. "Let's interview the cleaner first. Then Craig Logan."

Stella followed them down. She was eager for the opportunity to listen, take in protocols, and observe how the FBI conducted this in real life. Even though, when they entered the living room and came face to face with the distraught cleaner, all Stella wanted to do was take the slim, dark-haired woman in her arms.

She couldn't, of course. Clasping her hands behind her back, Stella hovered behind the men as they introduced themselves.

"Special Agent Roth, Special Agent Maxwell. Trainee agent Fall." Now that he was in an interview situation, Roth's hitherto concealed people skills were coming to the fore. "Ma'am, your name, please?" His voice was quiet and respectful.

"Cara Garcia," she said. She'd managed to get better control over her tears. Now, she looked blank-eyed, as if she had dissociated herself from the situation. Her hair had been tied up in a neat braid, but some of the strands had escaped and were sticking to her cheeks.

"Shall we sit?" Roth offered.

Cara folded back down onto the chaise lounge. Roth and Maxwell quickly carried two white, uncomfortable-looking designer chairs from other areas of the overly large room, and arranged them close by. Stella perched on the other end of the chaise lounge.

There was nobody else but them in the room. She guessed the police had shepherded Craig out of earshot while the interview took place.

"Please tell me some information about yourself." Roth's voice was soothing and calm. "Your role working for the Logans?"

"I was hired as a cleaner," Cara replied in a soft, trembling voice.

"How recently?"

"Today was supposed to be my first day," she confessed.

"That so?" Roth sounded surprised.

"I was interviewed last week by Mr. Logan," she said.

"Not by Amanda?" Roth asked. That would have been Stella's question, too, so she was interested in the answer.

"I arrived very early for the interview on Friday. I was going to wait outside until the time, but Mr. Logan was returning from a jog. He saw me and said he'd talk to me as his wife was still asleep. It was a short interview, as the agency I work for had sent through my CV and references. He seemed happy and said I could start today, being Wednesday."

"Were you replacing someone?"

Stella could see Cara thinking back.

"Yes. He said the cleaner employed by the previous owner had stayed on in the mornings, but yesterday was her last day as she was taking a flight back home."

A flight back home? On the day of the killing? Did that mean something? Stella wondered. She felt glad when Maxwell muttered, "We'll have to check that out."

"Okay. So you arrived this morning?" Roth continued.

"Yes. I was going to start at seven-thirty a.m. and was here a few minutes early."

"How did you get in?"

"The front door was unlocked. I knocked first, but when nobody answered, I wondered if they had left it open. Mr. Logan had said his wife would be there and that she would give me a key."

"So you got there, and you knocked, and then opened the door?"

"Yes."

Roth nodded. Stella guessed he was thinking of the open door and who could have left it unlocked. It pointed toward Amanda letting in someone she knew, although there were other possible scenarios. She could have forgotten to lock it and somebody had sneaked in. Or she could have been overpowered after unlocking it, and somebody had forced their way in.

"What did you see inside?" Roth asked Cara.

"It mostly looked the same as last time. I was interviewed here, in this room. Everything was tidy. I called out, said good morning, but there was no answer. I felt that something was wrong. Mrs. Logan should have been waiting for me. I decided I would go and look for her, and headed upstairs."

"You didn't go anywhere else in the house first?"

"No."

"Was the bedroom door open or closed?"

"It was partially open. I could already feel something wasn't right. I could smell the blood."

She drew in a hoarse gasp. Stella sensed her tears were threatening again.

"It must have been a shock," Roth said.

Cara rubbed her hands over her eyes and smoothed them down over her skirt, taking some time to gather herself.

"I was so shocked. It was like a nightmare."

"Did you notice any other details?" Maxwell asked in a gentle voice.

Cara thought again.

"A picture at the bottom of the stairs was knocked sideways. I straightened it, wondering if someone had hurried past, and if so, why. I have been in homes before that have been burgled," she said. "As soon as you walk in, you feel it. You see small things even if you do not notice them."

That was an important observation, Stella thought. Someone had hurried downstairs. Perhaps the killer, rushing out after doing the deed.

At any rate, Stella hadn't heard a note of discord in this account. It all made sense. She felt the cleaner had been truthful. Also it was unlikely she could have been involved, as such a recent employee.

Roth and Maxwell exchanged glances.

"Thank you for your time," Roth said. "I appreciate your help. We're done, and you can leave."

Looking relieved, Cara stood up and walked out.

Roth and Maxwell exchanged some quick, murmured comments.

"No problems with her version," Maxwell said.

"No. She confirmed the circumstances, but not otherwise involved."

They didn't consult with Stella, which felt weird after Quantico, which had been such a collaborative environment. Nobody was left out of a group discussion and everyone made sure to participate and give their input. Reluctantly, she supposed that school wasn't like real life. At any rate, she didn't need to say anything, because this had been a simple interview and they all agreed there were no more questions that could have been asked.

Grant hurried in, having obviously looked out for the cleaner's departure.

"Are you ready for Craig Logan?" he asked.

"We are. He can come in," Roth said.

This was going to be the more intense, and challenging, interview, Stella guessed. The spouse was always the main suspect, she knew from her training, even when things appeared to be perfect between them. She sat straighter as the door opened and Craig walked in.

CHAPTER SEVEN

As Craig walked in, Maxwell strode over to him and ushered him over to their impromptu interview setup. Stella thought he looked as if he needed the guidance. He was walking as if in a dream—or more probably a nightmare. His hair was ruffled, as if he hadn't brushed it. His shirt was creased, and looked like he'd slept in it. She couldn't tell if he'd shaved because he had a faint outline of designer stubble. He looked as if he'd seen a ghost.

"I don't know how this could have happened," he blurted out, as Maxwell helped him down onto the chaise lounge. "I just literally do not know. Amanda was the sweetest, kindest person. She had no enemies. She'd never have hurt anyone."

Again, he looked on the point of tears, but this time, in an interview situation, Stella found herself remaining more objective. Was his grief genuine? Crocodile tears could stream out if the stakes were high enough. She'd been taught that numerous times in the past four months.

She hoped the two agents would test his story and probe for any details that might shed a spark of light.

"When did you two meet?" Roth asked.

"Two years ago. At a work function. Amanda was with the event planning team," Craig said.

"And you got together after that?"

"Yes. Well, we connected instantly and we started dating a couple of weeks later. We were married the next year, on my thirtieth birthday."

This was all recent, Stella realized. Had there been enough time for the romance and fairy dust to wear off?

"When did you move here?" Roth asked.

"Two months ago. I was headhunted by Futureplus."

"And before that?"

"We lived in Hastings. I worked for my previous company for three years. No, sorry. Four years. It's all recorded on my CV and LinkedIn. Amanda worked until we moved here. She decided to take a break and get the house sorted. Then she was going to decide whether to look for something. Most probably she wouldn't have. There was no need. And we had talked about starting a family soon."

He rubbed a hand over his face.

Stella could see he was still in deep shock. She wondered how this would affect the accuracy of his answers. Certainly, he wasn't sure about dates and times.

"Did the move change the dynamic between you?" Roth asked.

"How do you mean?" Craig looked blank.

"Sometimes buying a new home or moving into a different environment can cause tension, fights, disruption. Do you recall anything like that?" Roth elaborated, staring intently at Craig.

"No. There was nothing like that. It was a positive move. We were both glad to be living here. It felt like an exciting adventure and fresh start. We had much more money to spend as I had a big salary increase with the move. Amanda actually chose this house. She loved it. And we hadn't had any fights before or during the move. The only problem was that we hadn't been spending a lot of time together with my working hours, but that was it."

Craig shook his head as if he couldn't work out how such a dream scenario had become a nightmare.

"Tell me about last night," Roth offered conversationally.

"I worked late and ended up sleeping at the office."

"Is that usual?" Roth asked.

"Yes, like I said, my job is very high pressure. I've had to make a lot of changes to the company's systems, I've had to procure updated equipment, and build relationships with a few new suppliers. Most of our contacts are in the Far East, so I've been traveling there regularly and it means my meetings are normally late night, to accommodate the time difference."

Now that he was talking in more general terms about his work, he seemed more coherent, as if he was able to slip into autopilot for a moment and forget about the terrible circumstances. Stella guessed he was a workaholic who'd immersed himself into his new role. Had that made a difference, or caused anything to go wrong? she wondered.

"So, sleeping over at the office. How often did it happen?" Roth said.

"Once or twice a week at the moment. I usually know by late afternoon if I'm going to be able to get home or not, and then I call Amanda. There's a pull-out sofa bed in my office. I keep a change of clothes there."

"So you called her in the afternoon?"

"No. I knew by lunch time I was going to have to work very late and might as well sleep over. I called her at around one or two p.m. and told her I'd see her tomorrow night."

"It was a short call?"

Craig looked briefly hunted, as if he suddenly feared a short call might be a bad thing.

"No, I mean, we spoke for a few minutes, I told her how work was going, she said she'd been out looking at…" He sighed, making a face. "Why can't I remember? Looking at furniture for the outdoor patio, I think. That was what she was doing."

"Did she sound normal?"

"Yes. Normal."

Stella saw Roth sit back, scribbling a few words on his notepad.

"Did she mention any visitors, anyone coming here?"

"No."

"Where are your offices?" Roth questioned. Stella guessed he wanted to know how far away they were. Could Craig have driven home and killed his wife?

At this stage, Stella wasn't sure if he could have done it or not. There was no way of knowing from his demeanor. Yes, he was shocked, but the act of murder was shocking in itself. His memory was imperfect, which could be an honest reaction after such a stressful event, but could equally be faked—or a result of the stress of killing her.

"They're ten miles away. In town."

Stella reckoned that at night, that would be a twenty-minute drive at most. Even taking a roundabout route, he could easily have gone there and back.

"And was anyone else working late with you?" Roth's next question proved he was thinking along the same lines.

"My assistant and two of the tech team worked until about seven. My assistant ordered me food before she left. Pizza. I ate it at my desk."

"Then, what time did you turn in?"

"I worked till after midnight. Put my head down, woke up at six, headed down to the gym for an hour. I was back in the office when the police called."

His voice dropped to a whisper.

"Your wife didn't contact you again?" Roth pressed.

"No. No, she didn't, but that was usual, too."

"Did you two have any friends nearby? How often did you socialize?"

Craig nodded. "We met the neighbors. We had dinner with them once. We went to a couple of my work events."

"Which neighbors?" Roth asked. Stella recalled that the home had neighbors on both sides, and a large park opposite.

"The Robsons. On our left. I don't know the people on the right."

"And during the day? Did Amanda have any activities, any clubs or hobbies?"

"She joined the gym. Did yoga classes. She'd met a couple of friends that she saw once or twice a week. I—I'm not totally sure of their names. Juliet was one, I think. The detectives have her phone, which was in her purse, and all the numbers will be on there."

Stella felt frustrated. So not even a phone or purse had been taken? It didn't sound like a break-in, and Amanda's life sounded innocent and normal. Where was the opportunity for emotions to flare in this easy, privileged routine?

"Was your wife, or anyone close to her, ever involved in drugs?" Maxwell then asked and Stella knew he was thinking of the other possible related case.

"Drugs?" Craig sounded surprised. "No. Not at all."

"Are you sure? No illegal substances whatsoever? And what about your close family?" Maxwell pressured.

"Amanda's an only child. My family's in Ohio, and none of them used or abused drugs. I don't even drink. Amanda would have wine with her friends but that's about it."

"Maybe check out the previous cleaner," Roth muttered, which Stella thought was a good idea. The cleaner's sudden departure was strange. If she'd had any illegal dealings going on the side, someone could have arrived looking to find her.

With that point made, Maxwell and Roth exchanged a meaningful glance that showed they were both racking their brains for any further loose ends, any inconsistencies that they could further test.

But they were coming up blank, from the short silence that followed.

As she thought about Amanda's evening routine, an important question suddenly occurred to Stella. Forgetting the dire warning Roth had given her about keeping her mouth shut, she cleared her throat and began speaking in a polite tone.

CHAPTER EIGHT

"Mr. Logan, can you tell me, did your wife—"

Stella stopped herself. This question was too abrupt, too personal. Rather, she should lead into it, but now she was out of time, because while Craig Logan had turned to stare at her, Roth's wrathful glare was already incinerating her.

Well, inappropriate as it was, she'd just have to blurt it out.

"I was wondering if Amanda usually went to bed with clothes on. I guess what I'm asking is, did she sleep in a nightshirt? Pajamas? Or naked?"

Now Roth's glare had intensified and Maxwell was adding his incredulous frown to the barrage of gazes turned her way.

"What kind of question is that?" Maxwell asked, his voice accusing.

Avoiding his gaze, Stella kept her own focused on Craig.

"Please, Mr. Logan, if you could just answer it."

Luckily, Craig seemed too unsettled to be bothered by the strangeness of it.

"She wore nightshirts," he said.

"Thank you," Stella replied.

Roth jumped to his feet. She could tell he was furious all over again with her.

"Thank you for your time, Mr. Logan. That concludes our questioning, and we won't need anything further today. We may have to interview you again, though."

Maxwell accompanied the trembling man to the door where the police were waiting. As soon as Craig was out, Roth turned to Stella, his face now brick red.

"What was that about?"

The incredulous tone of his voice said that he suspected her question was little more than time wasting, and that her answer had better be good.

"I had a thought and I wanted to follow it up, sir," Stella explained.

"Don't call me sir! I've told you once already! Are you listening to a thing I say?" he exploded at her, sounding at the end of his tether.

"I'm sorry, Roth," she apologized quickly, wanting to calm the situation down to rationality again. Roth could be surprisingly emotional, she realized.

"We all have thoughts, Fall. Some random. Others inappropriate. It doesn't mean we voice them during a key witness interview."

Stella waited for him to finish his rant. Then she stood her ground.

"I wouldn't ask a question if I didn't have a valid reason. I was brought in because I could offer insight. Unless I get the chance to speak up occasionally, I can't do it. So please can you respect that?"

Roth sighed. To her surprise, he didn't seem angry at her standing up for herself. Instead, it was as if she'd finally gotten him to listen to her side. He thought about her words and then gave a decisive nod.

"All right. Point taken. So, what is your reason?"

"I walked into the bathroom while we were upstairs. I noticed how clean the tub and shower were, and that there were no used bath towels. And that made me wonder why the victim was naked, because she hadn't just bathed."

Roth pressed his lips together while she spoke. She had no idea if he thought her theory had merit, or was complete nonsense.

"Did the killer undress her and take her clothes away? Are there any of her clothes missing? I can't figure out exactly how it happened."

From behind her, Stella heard an impatient throat clearing.

"Seriously? We're at a murder scene and you're worrying about the logistics of bathing and dressing?" There was incredulous amusement in Maxwell's tone. "I've heard some random theories in my time but I think this one wins it."

He glanced at Roth as if seeking confirmation that Stella was, undoubtedly, the most idiotic trainee agent ever to have been forcefully co-opted into an investigation.

But as Stella swiveled her worried glance toward Roth, she saw he was rubbing his chin thoughtfully.

"Yes. Your logic makes sense," he admitted, and Stella felt a rush of relief.

"The basin towel was wet. And there were water marks in there. That's what made me notice," she explained further.

"There's one way to find out. The coroner," Roth said. "They'll be able to confirm if there are any clothing fibers in the wounds."

There was a short silence. Stella sensed that Maxwell was struggling internally.

"All right," he snapped out, his face ruddier than she was used to seeing it. "I guess we go there next?"

"Could we not find out if there's any evidence of someone arriving during the evening?" Stella asked Roth, emboldened by this success.

"Were you not listening earlier? The home didn't have security in place."

Sticking to her original point, Stella persisted. "I know this home didn't. And the houses are large. But there are properties on either side that probably do have top-class security so maybe there's an overlap. One of them might have caught something on a side camera, or street camera? We could ask the neighbors if they saw anything, and if they didn't, whether we could access their security cameras."

Roth nodded decisively.

"Good point. Maxwell, you go around to the neighbors. Let's make contact, find out what they have. You can also interview the Robsons. When was this dinner Craig told us about? Did they have any further contact with Amanda after that?"

"I'll do that," Maxwell said, sounding extremely unhappy to be doing something that Stella had suggested.

"We'll head to the coroner in the meantime. Stella, come with me."

Talk about mixed emotions, Stella thought. She was vastly relieved that her theories hadn't been shot down and that Roth had, in fact, taken them seriously. At the same time, she could see she'd made an enemy out of Maxwell.

They climbed into the car again. It didn't feel any friendlier with just her and Roth, but Stella decided it was a modicum less hostile. She was glad of that, because going to the coroner would be another hurdle to overcome. They'd stood in on a postmortem during her academy training but that had been very different circumstances. It hadn't been a murder victim and it hadn't been someone who had died in a way similar to her fiancé. She was worried the trauma would surface again, and she was also fretting that she'd betray her lack of experience. She had no idea what to look out for in a postmortem.

She felt green, inexperienced, and out of her depth.

*

After a twenty-minute drive, Roth pulled up outside the forensic pathology laboratory. While immersed in her own worried thoughts, Stella had noticed the landscape changing as they'd headed into a more industrial side of town. Chic, treed suburbia had been replaced by modern office parks and warehouses. Roth parked outside a red brick building with discreet signage outside. After signing in with security at the gate, it was opened, and they headed across the paved courtyard for another security check at the main door.

Clearly familiar with the building's layout, Roth then headed briskly down a corridor. Stella followed, striding in his wake. As she reached the double doors at the end of the corridor, she picked up the acrid scent of strong disinfectant, underlain by an almost undetectable organic aroma.

Roth pressed a buzzer and waited for the doors to be opened. Inside, there was another reception desk where an attendant in a green jacket was stationed.

A long corridor led off this central area and Stella saw doors at intervals, each one closed. She guessed that in such an environment, each unit had to be self-contained to avoid cross-contamination.

"Which room is the Logan postmortem in?" he asked.

"Sign in here, please, sir." The attendant handed him a register. "The protective clothing is in the cupboard on your right. You can go to room five."

After masking up and pulling on gloves and protective gowns, they headed down the corridor to the room, where Roth tapped on the door. After a pause, it was opened by a masked, gowned man with an ID tag pinned to his shirt.

"Roth!"

"Glenn."

Roth turned to Stella. "This is Spencer Glenn, a senior pathologist. This is trainee agent Stella Fall."

"I just finished the postmortem. Do you want to take a look?" Glenn asked.

Roth glanced at Stella. She guessed he was checking to see if she was up for this. She nodded, and they walked into the room.

The brightly lit room was scrupulously clean. Amanda's body was laid out on a steel table and had been covered with a sheet. Glenn drew back the sheet and Stella walked over.

Emotions flooded through her as she stared down at the woman's still, pale face. A perfect, porcelain oval, framed by russet hair. Seeing her naked body felt like a violation, but a bigger insult was the multiple stab marks that slashed into her chest and stomach. They looked even worse than the major incisions that the pathologist had neatly made during his examination.

Stella could only imagine the bloodbath it must have been when her body was brought in. Now cleaned, the wounds looked stark and terrible.

"There are nine stab marks, made by a medium-sized and very sharp blade that fits the description of the missing kitchen knife. This was the fatal one, which pierced her heart and killed her instantly," Glenn explained.

"Was it the first one?" Roth asked, and Stella knew he was also imagining the bloody, violent scene that had played out in that immaculate white bedroom.

"No. Probably the second or third one, given the defensive wounds on her right palm and also a cut along her wrist."

"That's harsh," Roth muttered, and Stella glanced at him, surprised by the first hint of real humanity she'd seen from him.

"From the angle of these cuts, I'm guessing that our killer is right-handed," Roth then said, peering down.

"Unfortunately, I agree with you," Glenn said reluctantly.

As she looked, and as Roth pointed out the details with careful, gloved fingers, Stella could see how the driving force behind the blade was definitely from the right side. Luckily, the logistics behind the attack were fascinating enough to distract her mind from the grim reality of what they were examining so closely.

She'd been worried about getting dizzy or nauseous but she found her mind was too preoccupied to allow for that as she gazed at the corpse.

"If she died instantly after the second or third blow, why do you think the killer kept going?" Roth asked her.

There was only one explanation, chilling as it was.

"I guess it must be because he, or she, was angry. He was in a fury. He didn't want to stop. So it was a crime of hatred or passion," she said.

"I agree," Roth said. "So either someone had a serious personal grudge, or else Amanda was the extremely unlucky victim of a violent break-in."

"Without any sign of a forced entry or anything stolen," Stella added.

"Exactly," Roth said in frustration.

"Are there any cloth fibers in the wounds?" he asked Glenn.

"No. No evidence of any clothing fibers."

Roth nodded, and Stella guessed that meant her theory was right.

"Time of death?"

"Estimated between eight and ten p.m. Could have been earlier, but probably not later."

"Stomach contents?" Roth asked.

"There's evidence she ate a light meal an hour previously. Also, the toxicology shows she had a blood alcohol level of point oh-nine," Glenn continued.

So she'd eaten and drunk a couple of glasses of wine or some other alcoholic drink. Stella felt mystified. It had been a normal evening, until it hadn't anymore.

"Any other evidence?"

"Nothing." Glenn shrugged. "I wish there was more. But that's what we have."

Thanking Glenn, they stepped out of the room. Roth led the way back through the building, its hushed, bustling, disinfectant-scented interior leaving a lasting impression on Stella. She was grateful to climb back into the leather-lined safety of the car.

"It must have been someone who knew her," Roth said, as they headed out of the premises. They turned in a different direction at the main road, so Stella guessed they were headed for the local precinct, to collate the evidence they had so far.

"I think it was the husband," Stella said. "The spouse is always the prime suspect in these cases, aren't they?"

Roth glanced at her. "That's a big assumption to make, considering he has an alibi."

"But does he?" Stella argued. "He could have come back home and found her with someone else. That would fit in with a crime of passion. Maybe after that, he went back to the office and pretended he'd been there all along. He could even have paid his assistant to say he was there all the time."

She could see the scenario playing out, clear in her mind. His shock as he'd realized what was happening. The other man bolting for the door. And then turning to her, angrily, filled with rage.

Wait. One stumbling block.

Where had he gotten the knife from? It wasn't like a knife would be lying around in that tidy bedroom. And the kitchen and dining room were a long way away.

Stella revised her theory.

He'd stormed downstairs in pursuit of the fleeing lover. That would make sense. He'd detoured to the kitchen, grabbed a knife with the intention of killing the other man, and sprinted after him. But by that time, the lover was long gone. Ran away, hid, got into his car and sped off, who knew?

So then, with knife in hand and emotions boiling over, Craig had stormed back upstairs to confront his wife. And then, his rage had taken over and he hadn't been able to control himself.

But Roth's chastising words interrupted Stella's train of thought.

"Be careful about jumping to conclusions based on your own ideas, when the evidence doesn't lead you there. At best, that theory is flimsy. The simplest explanation is not always the right one when it comes to a crime. We have to follow the clues and see where they lead."

Stella drew breath to explain more about her theory but she was met by Roth's warning frown.

"Don't allow your own feelings to derail the investigation. It's what every new agent does. Let the evidence guide you," he said sternly.

Reminded of her lowly status, Stella backed down. She could see Roth's point. She was trying to pull the evidence her way, twist it to fit in with her logic. But she had to step back and instead of shaping it, she must follow it, faint and frustrating as the trail was. It was the correct way.

"I'm sorry, Roth," she said, and saw his surprised glance. He'd expected her to be more arrogant. Well, she was here to learn and needed to pick up on her mistakes quickly.

Even so, she couldn't help stashing the idea away in the back of her mind. Perhaps new evidence would come to light that might prove it true.

"Now, let's head to the police station. We'll set up shop there and go through the evidence we've found so far. And, Fall, once we're there, I have an important job for you."

CHAPTER NINE

Glancing around as Roth parked outside the Fairfield police precinct building, Stella was reminded again that this was a wealthy and upmarket part of the world. She thought the quaint, well-kept building, with its symmetrical frontage, Georgian architecture, and manicured planters outside, looked surprisingly pretty and welcoming.

Inside was more traditional, with the impersonal bustle that she expected to see. A short line of people were waiting at the help desk. Wooden benches lined the walls, while the area beyond was glassed off.

Roth walked to a side door, which the desk sergeant buzzed open as he reached it. He pushed it open and headed down a long corridor lined with doors. She heard the click of computer keys, the rustle of paper, the incessant crackle of walkie-talkies.

At the end of the corridor was a large, open-plan office with three big desks, ranks of filing cabinets, and two overstuffed bookshelves. The walls were plastered with framed certificates, taped circulars, and a few poster-size images of sports cars.

Testosterone oozed from every crevice. Stella felt like an outsider in this dominantly male space.

Two detectives were poring over a laptop at the right-hand desk. And, as Stella greeted them with a friendly hello, a side door opened and Maxwell walked in with another detective wearing a shirt and tie.

"We got back half an hour ago," he said to Roth. "I interviewed both sets of neighbors and we've been examining the footage next door."

"What did the neighbors say?" Roth asked.

Maxwell shook his head. "Unfortunately, the neighbors who knew the Logans were away on vacation until today. They had just come back from a week away when I arrived, and were unpacking the car, complete with their five-year-old twins and family dog. So there was nobody home at the time of the murder, although they gave me the camera footage. It'll probably take another half hour to go through it all. Want to sit in?" he invited Roth.

"I'll sit in," Roth agreed. "And the other neighbors?"

"Middle-aged folk who keep to themselves. They didn't know the Logans at all. They gave me a copy of their camera footage, too."

"I'll come through now. Fall, in the meantime, this is the job I need you to do."

"Sure," Stella said, wondering what it was going to be.

Roth indicated the other side of the desk in the far corner.

"Make yourself some space there. I'm going to give you everything we have, so far, on the other murder in Waterbury. I want you to look through it and pick up on the similarities. We need to assess whether it may, in fact, be a serial case."

Stella felt pleased to be given this job, which sounded like a challenge as well as a responsibility. She now knew quite a lot about the Logan killing, but very little about the other one. She remembered Roth had said it had taken place just a couple of days ago. Already, she felt unsure, as this was a short interval for a serial killer.

She sat down and Roth placed a thick case file in front of her, before disappearing next door.

Though spacious, the office smelled musty, as if years and years of paperwork had infused themselves in the air. And, though neat, she guessed that the ranks of filing cabinets lining the walls were stuffed with files on cases old and new, solved and unsolved. She felt weirdly reassured to be at work in exactly the environment where her father would have spent much of his working life.

Opening the file, Stella got ready to immerse herself in a brand new case history. Would there be any similarities or clues? Had the same modus operandi been used?

As she paged through, she learned that the murder two days ago had taken place in a different neighborhood. Scanning the area map, Stella noticed much smaller properties. This was not a highly affluent area but rather a more ordinary suburb.

The murder had occurred in the early evening. The victim, a thirty-year-old divorcée, had lived alone. Stella noted the similarity in ages. Was that a clue?

Another similarity was that there was no sign of forced entry. She felt her spine prickle with excitement as she read on. Could this be the start of a serial killing spree?

As she looked at the diagram of the stab wounds, she paused. The woman had been stabbed three times in the chest by a right-handed assailant. She'd been clothed at the time and when found, had been slumped in the hallway of her home.

Three times versus nine? That was an escalation. Doubtful now, she pressed on.

The victim was currently unemployed, she learned. She'd been fired from her job as a hotel receptionist after being caught stealing money from the till.

Prior to that, she'd been arrested for possession of drugs, but there hadn't been sufficient evidence to convict her.

This was painting a very different picture, Stella decided. She had a feeling that this unfortunate victim had become involved in the world of drugs and had been stealing to support her habit. Given that, she could have been stabbed by a dealer, or by someone she was buying off or borrowing from.

The photos of the house, where the woman had been found dead in the hallway, confirmed Stella's ideas. The house was not well maintained. The front yard looked wild and untended. The door had dents and splinters as if some other angry person had tried to kick it in previously.

Although this didn't look like a copycat murder, it did remind Stella that the drugs angle hadn't been ruled out. It was something to be aware of even though there had been no sign of them in Amanda's toxicology report.

If drugs were somehow a common thread, perhaps through the previous cleaner being involved and having attracted trouble to the home, then the two killings could possibly be linked. Otherwise, there were no signs of it being a typical serial crime.

At that moment, Roth hurried back in.

Stella organized her thoughts, hoping that she'd be able to get this important information across as clearly as possible—and that she hadn't missed any details.

"Roth, I don't think it's a serial. They're too different. The only similarities are the stabbings, and even there, there's no sign of the same crazy anger in this earlier killing. However, we can't rule out drugs, and that there might be a common factor between the two deaths as a result."

She'd hoped that Roth might be impressed by her analysis. However, she wasn't prepared for his impatient nod.

"Yes, yes. I know."

"You know?" Stella had hoped her insights would have been better received.

Bursting her bubble completely, Roth continued. "I already went over the files and reached the same conclusion. I gave it to you as a test. I'm glad you picked up on the possibility of drugs in the Logans' scenario, and I agree we need to keep considering a common thread there. But now you need to come next door, because we have footage from the neighbor's camera of a vehicle arriving at their house in the late afternoon."

Stella's miffed feeling dissolved at this news.

"A vehicle arriving at the Logans'?"

"Yes," Roth said, and despite the terse reply, Stella could pick up he was as excited as she now felt.

She jumped to her feet and hurried through to the next door room, where a big-screen TV was set up. There were several chairs and desks in the small space. She perched on one of them and Roth took another.

Maxwell was tapping his fingers on the video remote, looking impatient, as if he already wanted to make an arrest.

"The Robsons have two cameras on their property, and one has a panoramic view of the road. The time stamp is accurate. They're not always, but I checked. See here. At six p.m."

"That's at least an hour before the time of death," Roth muttered as Maxwell ran the video.

"Coroner did say it could have been earlier," Maxwell argued.

Stella watched carefully. The footage was clear and crisp, from a good quality cam. In color, too. The grass looked lurid green, the edge of the street sooty black, the paved driveway golden beige.

"Watch carefully here."

Stella leaned forward in her seat. What would she see?

There it was. She held her breath as the gleaming silver car hood edged into view. It was a Mercedes, she saw. It swung right, entering the next-door driveway, but as it did so, for a moment, the number plate was visible.

"Wait again," Maxwell breathed.

He fast-forwarded. Not for long. Stella watched the time stamp carefully. Barely five minutes later, the car drove out again. It was a little darker now and the rear indicator blinked brightly as it turned into the road.

"Have you traced the plate?" Stella asked.

"We have." Maxwell sounded caught up in the thrill of the chase.

"Who does it belong to?"

He gave her a satisfied smile. "Craig Logan."

Stella nearly fell off her chair.

The husband had come home in the late afternoon? He'd sworn he'd been at work the entire day. Not once had he mentioned driving home.

He'd lied, and his presence at the crime scene—even if slightly earlier than the time of death indicated—was highly incriminating.

Did this mean they had found their killer?

CHAPTER TEN

Half an hour later, Stella watched as Detective Grant hurried into the office, closely followed by a pale-faced Craig. She thought he looked even more haunted and stressed than he had the first time she had seen him. Her heart quickened as she realized this could be evidence of his guilt.

"Why am I here?" Panicked and thrown, Craig was babbling. "Am I being arrested? What is this about?"

He must know, Stella thought. Surely he knew? Or was he pretending innocence?

"Mr. Logan, we have a question for you. We'd like you to watch this video footage, taken from the neighbor's camera."

"Sure."

Craig followed the agents into the video room. He sat down on the edge of his chair, fingers drumming the desk. An expectant frown creased his forehead.

Detective Grant sat next to him and watched him closely. Stella guessed he was keeping ready for any violent reaction.

Weirdly, Craig seemed to have no idea what was coming.

The video played out in its lurid, colored silence.

As the car departed, Craig said suddenly, "Wait, that's my car. It's my car on the film?"

"The footage is from yesterday afternoon. Check out the time stamp," Roth said heavily.

Craig was still looking confused. So much so that Stella was starting to wonder if someone else had taken his car. And then, horrified realization dawned in his eyes.

"It's me," he said, his voice shaking.

Stella felt on the edge of her seat with tension as she watched his reactions, taking in his confusion and his evident fear.

"You told us you were at the office all day yesterday," Roth said in the same implacable voice.

"I was! I was, but I totally forgot I came home. I'd left my phone charger in the bedroom. I'd—I'd just gotten a new phone. I can show you the messages that said they were delivering it on Monday. The charger at the office wasn't compatible. I knew I'd need it so I raced home to get it. I went back again right away. My assistant can confirm. She brought me the pizza after I was back."

He was looking stunned, and also frightened. Was that because he was guilty?

His next words proved otherwise.

"I can't believe I forgot that. How did I forget to tell you? I swear, I'm telling the truth, I didn't mean to leave it out. It's like it just got wiped from my mind."

Stella found his reaction disappointingly plausible. His fear at the memory loss seemed totally genuine, and she could imagine that due to stress, certain things would just be dumped from his memory.

But he could be acting, simply redirecting his fear of being caught out, she reminded herself. He was a highly intelligent man, after all.

"Where was Amanda when you arrived home?" Roth asked.

"She wasn't there. She had a yoga class. She goes two afternoons a week. I literally just ran upstairs, grabbed the charger, ate an apple, and headed out again."

"Do you have an alibi for last night between eight and ten p.m.?" Roth asked.

Craig nodded. His hands were shaking violently.

"I was in videoconferences with our suppliers in Hong Kong and Indonesia. From seven p.m. to midnight, pretty much nonstop, I think my longest break was ten minutes. They were all recorded. I can pull up the recordings for you."

"Please do," Roth said sternly, but the cutting edge was gone from his voice, and Stella could see he believed him. Craig had an alibi, even if it was still to be double-checked. His reason for coming back seemed innocent and the fact he'd forgotten to mention it was plausible in the circumstances. This was not their suspect—at any rate, not yet. They needed to keep looking.

But even so, Stella hated having to let go of him again.

"I'll need those recordings by first thing tomorrow," Roth insisted.

Craig hesitated. "There are some very confidential issues being discussed," he said.

Roth pressed his lips together. "You can count on the FBI's confidentiality when it comes to a murder case," he said. "We're not in the business of selling secrets."

"Of course."

"You may go now. The officer will walk you out."

The police detective got up and accompanied Craig out of the video room.

As soon as he'd left, Roth said to Maxwell, "We'd better confirm that Amanda was at yoga. Do you have the details of the class she took?"

"Yes. It's a local instructor who lives a couple of blocks away. I'll call her now."

He looked through his notes before picking up the phone and dialing. Then he grimaced. "She's not answering."

In the meantime, Stella turned her attention back to the footage. They'd only watched a ten-minute segment of it, but there were a few hours saved on the tape.

Surely someone else might have arrived?

But as she watched it, Stella realized its limitations. It only showed the cars arriving and leaving from the left side of the Logans' house. They'd been lucky that Craig had arrived from that direction. But she remembered that Maxwell had obtained footage from the other side too.

"What's the tape from the other neighbors like?" she asked.

"We got it, but it's basically useless. The cameras on the other house only show their driveway and the edge of the road," Roth said, sounding as frustrated as Stella now felt. "We'll send it to our tech team in New Haven and see if there's any detail they can pick up."

"Can I look now, while it's here?" she asked.

"Sure," he said.

Stella uploaded the footage. This home had a poorer quality security system. The footage was grainier, in black and white rather than color. And although cars passed by on the road, all that could be seen was a tantalizing glimpse of them. No plates were visible.

Stella fast-forwarded to the time of the murder and then worked back, going slowly. Perhaps there would be a detail. A car might have swerved. She wasn't going to abandon hope.

And then she saw it. Not a car, but a person.

A grainy image of someone walking past quickly, hands in jacket pockets and head bowed. As the figure reached the edge of the image, it veered left, as if he was turning into the next door house's driveway.

"Hey! Look here!" she called.

In a moment, Roth was by her side.

"What we got?" he said, sounding enthused.

"A pedestrian. Not a car. And they arrived at eight, which is exactly in the murder's timeframe."

“A pedestrian. Interesting,” Roth said.

Stella added, “I recently stayed in a neighborhood similar to this one.” She saw Maxwell’s head turn sharply and his disapproving glare. So, as she’d sensed, he had a grudge against her because he assumed she’d wangled her way onto this case through influential connections, rather than earned it through merit and experience.

That was totally wrong, but there was no time to correct him now.

“I was only there for a few days. But that was one of the things I noticed. If people were out, it was because they were exercising—running, dog walking, pushing a stroller. People didn’t just walk. They drove.”

“Good point,” Roth said.

“Surely it might have been the killer?” Stella said.

“The timing works. But if this is all we have, we can’t tell anything from it.”

Maxwell squinted up at the screen.

“Looks like a man to me,” he said. “Wearing pants and a dark jacket.”

“Could just as easily be a woman,” Roth argued. “Without anyone else to compare it to, or anyone for scale, you can’t tell.”

“Man or woman, he or she definitely looked headed to the Logans’ house.”

Stella’s eyes felt as if they were watering as she ran and reran the clip, not daring to blink in case she missed anything.

It was such a short moment. A few purposeful steps in the right direction at the right time. If only they had more detail. How exquisitely frustrating it was to be looking at what might have been the killer arriving. Was there another way to get more information? she wondered, feeling driven to explore any solutions.

Maxwell clearly felt the same.

“We need to pull other footage from houses further up the road,” he suggested.

Roth sighed. “We can, but I fear it will be a waste of time. This person was only in the camera frame for a moment because he, or she, was turning into the Logans’ home. They could have walked alongside the park on the opposite side of the road, and in fact probably did, and crossed the road as they reached the house. Wouldn’t you choose to do that, if you were arriving somewhere where you didn’t want to be seen?”

Maxwell nodded reluctantly.

"And they could have parked their car anywhere in the area, or even taken a bus." Roth sounded frustrated as he checked his watch.

At that moment, Stella's phone rang. It was a number she didn't recognize.

"Excuse me," she said, and hurried out of the office to answer the call.

"As soon as she picked up, she heard Carrie's voice, loud and victorious.

"Stella Fall? It's me, Carrie. Where are you? Are you coming back tonight?"

Stella's gut clenched. Suddenly, all the progress she'd made today and the steep learning curve she'd embarked on felt pointless.

This woman could end her career whenever she chose, and Stella had a strong suspicion that she was going to choose to as soon as she possibly could.

"I'm not going to be back tonight," she said. "I've been asked to help out the FBI office in New Haven with an investigation."

There was a stunned pause. Stella could feel the resentment radiating from the other end of the line.

"They're using you?" Jealousy blazed from her words.

"I have relevant experience," Stella stated calmly.

"The only way they should be using you is as an example of how not to do things. And if they aren't already, they will be soon." Now Carrie's voice resonated with triumph. "I wonder if they know that the trainee agent helping them has had a formal complaint of assault laid against her this afternoon, lodged at the director's office? I was badly hurt in the fall when you attacked me, which prevented me finishing the obstacle course. I had to receive medical attention for it. Marc is following up on this as we speak. You're not going to graduate, Stella Fall. What you did to me today will mean the end of your career!"

"Wait!" Stella cried. Had she really sprained her wrist in the fall? Stella's memory was that she'd landed squarely on her butt. Her mind raced as she stared desperately around the cream-tiled corridor, with its official notices on the walls. It didn't matter how she'd hurt herself, Stella decided. She was going to have to apologize, whatever it took and no matter what Carrie wanted her to say.

But the line was dead. Stella felt sick as she stared down at her phone, confirming the call had disconnected.

Quickly Stella called back, feeling her heart accelerate as she got through to Carrie's voicemail.

“Please call me urgently,” she said. “Or I’ll try to call you later.”

She felt wrung out by anxiety over this. Carrie knew she held all the power and she was going to get her revenge.

This would be her first, and only, case with the FBI.

What should she do now? she agonized, as she headed back inside. She had no idea whether to spill her predicament to Roth, or at least forewarn him, or whether it would be better to tough it out and hope that the bombshell only landed after the case was over.

There wasn’t a moment to waste in solving this crime. The clock was ticking for her, in more ways than one.

CHAPTER ELEVEN

As she trailed back into the office, Stella had another thought. Perhaps she could plead for clemency with Marc, and explain that Carrie had been about to grab her first.

But as the thought occurred to her, she shook her head. Nobody else would have seen the moment when Carrie clenched her fists. Stella had acted too quickly in her own defense. Plus, there had been witnesses to her attack. She'd even heard one of the guys say, "Oof," in an amused way as it had happened.

Witnesses would seal her fate and she felt furious with herself for that one reckless moment. Why, oh why, had she allowed Carrie to provoke her? Just a few more days and she'd never have had to see her again.

She felt wrung out by guilt and regret. After the craziness of the day, this bombshell made her want to burst into tears.

Was there anyone else she could contact to plead her case. Clem, perhaps? Would he be able to intervene? More to the point, Stella wondered miserably, would he be willing to intervene?

She'd brought this upon herself, and couldn't impose upon her mentor to try and save her from the consequences.

Inside the office, Roth and Maxwell were deep in discussion.

"It's nearly six p.m. now, and we've been able to get an appointment to interview another witness at seven. I'm going to call the New Haven office and update them on progress so far. You two might as well head out and have a bite to eat, because who knows how late we'll end up working? Take the car. You've got an hour. No longer."

Stella glanced dubiously at Maxwell. This wasn't what she'd wanted. She'd rather have gone and foraged for herself. But the police station was located in suburbia and there didn't look to be anywhere close by in this unfamiliar area.

From the way Maxwell glared at her, she could see he wasn't thrilled with Roth's decision either, and would rather have headed out on his own, too.

They walked out of the police station and climbed into the car in silence. The weather matched Stella's mood. It was cloudy and dull, with a mist of drizzle in the air.

Maxwell clearly knew his way around the area well. He drove to the bottom of a main street that looked to be busy with smart restaurants, bars, and exclusive stores. In this gloomy evening, the lights looked bright and welcoming.

"There's a burger bar up here that I like," he said.

Stella felt relieved. A burger sounded like a good choice. Simple, substantial, and full of calories. She realized she was starving. She'd had an arduous day and she hadn't eaten since early that morning at the FBI academy, when she'd wolfed down a single piece of toast before heading to the exam room.

The bar was buzzing with early evening trade. Rock music thudded and boomed from the open doors. There were a few tables on the sidewalk, all full. Maxwell headed inside and Stella followed, blasted by the mouthwatering aroma of charred burger, overlaid with the smell of beer.

He walked purposefully to a small corner table and they sat down.

"One special double-decker cheeseburger meal, with a side of large fries," Maxwell said.

"Make that two, please. And a big bottle of water," Stella added. She needed to hydrate after her long, tiring day.

Stella had thought that the restaurant would be too noisy for any coherent conversation, because the volume level was increasing by the minute, but squashed together at the tiny table, they were so close by that hearing each other wasn't a problem. It was more of a challenge to think what to say.

Luckily, the waitress returned almost immediately with the water. Stella took a large, grateful gulp. Now that her thirst was quenched, she was even hungrier, she realized.

Sitting opposite Maxwell was the closest she'd been to him all day. Her view had otherwise mostly been of the back of his head in the car, coupled with the occasional glare during the interviews. Now she saw he had an earring hole in his left ear, and some sort of a silver ring on a leather thong around his neck, half-hidden by his now unfastened collar.

And his eyes were a light, golden brown.

She had no idea what to say to him. Maxwell was the first to start the conversational ball rolling, to her relief.

"So. Your first day on a real case. What did you make of it?"

"It was more stressful than I expected. I've been—" Quickly, she stopped herself. She'd been about to share with Maxwell that she'd been personally caught up in a murder. Waking up next to a bloody corpse and being a prime suspect was just about as close as could be. But she didn't want to speak about that. She was reluctant to talk about herself at all. Maxwell thought she was so different from what she was. He had no idea of her small-town upbringing, the tough early life she'd had, the devastating disappearance of her father that had reshaped her world.

Maxwell thought she'd gotten invited into this case as a result of connections up top, and her friendship with Clem. Well, let him think so. It was a hundred percent safer. She'd only be here another day at most.

She changed what she was going to say.

"I don't feel I know Amanda, the victim, at all. It's like she's an unknown entity and I feel I need to know her if we're going to find out what happened."

Maxwell was looking at her with puzzlement.

"That's not what I thought you'd say."

"Why?" Had she said something wrong? Stella wondered.

"Most people would be looking at the evidence, and seek more information. You're trying to find out about who she was," he explained.

Stella made a face.

"I'm not experienced yet. But my background is psychology. I studied forensic psychology. So I guess that's why I default to that."

Maxwell shook his head. "I guess it's helpful to have a different perspective, but I feel desperate for more evidence. That's what my background is telling me," he said, giving a quick smile.

"Tell me about your background," Stella said, taking the opportunity to steer the questions away from herself.

"It's science and IT. I have a master's in data science. I worked in the IT industry for five years, in New York City."

Stella was impressed. That sounded skilled and high-powered.

"Where did you study?" she asked.

"Cornell University. I got a scholarship there," he said.

"Why did you join the FBI?" she asked, wondering what had prompted such a drastic career move.

"One of the board of execs in the firm where I worked was laundering money for a criminal connection."

"Oh, wow, really?" Stella was fascinated to learn this. "What happened?"

"The FBI agents came in to investigate. Two agents spent about a week going through the company's finances and systems."

"Were you a suspect?" Stella asked.

Maxwell shook his head. "No, but they had to work with our team in order to access the systems and pinpoint if there was anything going on."

"Did they find anything?" she asked.

"He'd run it through three other companies that he was also involved in, but we were able to pull up some of the evidence through our systems."

"So working with them made you want to join?"

"Yes. I spent a lot of time with them, and by the end I was hugely motivated to join."

"Why was that?"

"I guess it seemed so purposeful. I was earning well in my job, had a corner office by the age of twenty-seven, the whole package—but these guys were making a difference I could never make. They encouraged me to apply. Said there was a need for agents with my skill set. So I took the plunge."

He looked away as he spoke, and Stella sensed there was more. From the way his gaze had slipped sideways, Maxwell had other reasons for making the decision.

Intrigued by this clue that his body language offered, Stella couldn't help but pursue it.

"Did you have to relocate?" she asked.

"Yes. I moved from New York after training, when they assigned me to the New Haven office."

"That must have been disruptive. Did you make other changes in your life?"

"Of course. I made a lot of changes." Now he seemed more defensive, as if there was a topic he didn't want to broach.

She had a handle on his body language now. There was something else. Something personal.

He glanced down at his left hand, and suddenly she knew.

"Relationship changes?" she asked. He'd broken up with someone who'd been serious. Either a fiancée, or he'd gone through a divorce.

She wondered if that had provided an additional reason for him to take the leap into a new life and join the FBI.

Maxwell stared at her. He looked surprised, and she saw a flash of anger in his eyes.

Suddenly, there was tension between them that hadn't been there before.

And then, surprisingly, Maxwell laughed.

"You're profiling me," he said. "Stop it. I'm not a suspect."

Stella laughed, too. "I'm sorry. I can't help it. My background's psychology and it's what I do."

"You need to separate work from after-hours," he warned, and she sensed he was not joking.

Their food arrived. Stella's mouth watered at the tasty-looking double-decker burgers, with sides of golden fries. She still couldn't believe that she'd started off the morning at Quantico, expecting a normal day. Now she was here, thrown into an important investigation.

Tomorrow she might go back to the academy to face a disciplinary hearing. Suddenly, Stella wished this case would never be solved. She didn't want what was coming next.

Not even the trouble that she was going to be in could affect her appetite. She was far too hungry for that. She attacked the burger, craving every bite of the juicy, fatty calories it provided.

"Does it ever get easier?" she asked him.

"Does what get easier?"

"Separating work from after-hours."

He thought for a while. "No. Honestly, not so far for me. It doesn't. But you have to try. You have to set your professional life aside and keep it separate. Especially with some of the cases you'll be involved in," he warned.

"When did you join?" she asked.

"I joined the academy this time last year," Maxwell said.

That meant eight months' experience under his belt as well as the four months of training. That accounted for his abrasive attitude toward her. He was the new agent on the block and wanted to prove himself.

Plus, coming from a science and data background would mean he had excellent analytic skills. People skills, perhaps not so much. Maybe that had been the area Maxwell had needed to work on at the academy, she thought, with an inward smile. It clearly wasn't his strong suit and now, at least, she could see the reason for it.

She put her knife and fork together, having finished every crumb.

“I guess we’d better head back and pick up Roth,” Maxwell said, waving to get the check. “I’ll pay. It’s on expenses anyway. You might as well save your money.”

“Okay. Thanks.”

He handed over a few ten-dollar bills and pocketed the check. Then she stood up and followed him out of the now-packed restaurant.

As she climbed into the car, she felt glad to have learned more about Maxwell. Hopefully, this quick meal had eased his initial distrust of her. It would make it easier to work with him on the rest of this case.

She felt eager to tackle another witness interview that might shed more light on the puzzling circumstances of this gruesome murder.

CHAPTER TWELVE

Stella thought that Roth looked stressed as he climbed into the back of the car. His next words confirmed it.

"We're under the gun here. We're being pressured by the Fairfield town council. They don't want the national media getting hold of this case. With this type of murder, and the level of violence involved, it will be hugely detrimental to property values and tourism in the area. They need it solved as soon as possible. They've pleaded for us to stay on it, keep assisting the police, and get it wrapped up fast."

"Hopefully the next interviews will give us something. Plus, there's still the drugs angle to consider, possibly with the previous cleaner's involvement," Maxwell observed. "From my experience in other cases, I think that could play a role."

"We haven't been able to contact the cleaner. The phone number Craig gave us is no longer operational and she moved out of her lodgings on her last day of work," Roth said.

"That's significant," Maxwell said, and Stella agreed. This was sounding suspicious.

"My team is trying to locate the previous owners of the home, to see if they have any alternative numbers for her," Roth said.

As they headed on a zigzag route into the suburbs, Stella hoped she could contribute some value to the next interview. Perhaps approaching it from the psychology side could speed up the investigation. She resolved to pick up as much as she possibly could about the characters and personalities of Amanda's friends and contacts.

"This interview is with Juliet Brand, a friend of the victim. Juliet said the group of four friends got together for a bridge game a couple of times a week," Roth said.

"A bridge game," Maxwell repeated, sounding amused. Stella guessed it was a big step away from the drugs scenario he'd been thinking of.

"It goes with the territory," Roth agreed. "In this area, many of the housewives spend their time doing shopping, yoga, beauty treatments, and bridge is very popular."

Stella was wondering what Amanda had thought of these circumstances. She'd been thrown into a brand new environment. Had the new lifestyle brought any other changes or mind shifts along with it? she wondered. She hoped the interview ahead would offer some clues.

Something had changed. Something had snapped. A situation had been created where murder had been done.

She knew evidence was important. But in her experience of a similar crime, the key lay in the feelings, the emotions. In uncovering the secrets and dynamics that had led up to that bloody, violent moment.

How could she find out what they had been?

"Here we are," Roth said. He parked outside a beautiful home that Stella guessed was in the same wider neighborhood as Amanda's mini-palace, even though they'd taken a different route there and she didn't recognize the road. This home looked more established. The front yard was flanked with beautiful flower beds. There was even a stone statue near the ornamental fishpond on the left of the house. Stella distinctly heard Maxwell snort as he saw that statue.

They opened the garden gate and headed up to the front door. Juliet must have seen their headlights outside, because she opened it as they arrived.

She was a pretty, slim brunette with long, wavy hair, who looked to be around Amanda's age. Stella noted, with a quick glance, that she was perfectly made up, immaculately manicured, and wearing a cream top and tan pants that were elegant in an understated way. Stella guessed her home would be the same.

There was a faint air of anxiety about her which Stella sensed immediately.

"Officers, good evening." She looked serious and worried as she ushered them in. "I'm Juliet Brand. Please come this way."

The living room where she showed them into was simplistically elegant, with pale gray leather couches, pastel art on the walls, and a huge glass window overlooking the large back yard. Stella thought this décor might very much reflect Juliet's personality.

"Can I offer you tea? Coffee? I have both waiting in the kitchen. My husband is going to be working late tonight, so you'll only be speaking to me. Does that matter? He's never met Amanda."

"It's no problem, ma'am. And I'd like coffee, please," Roth said, and Stella and Maxwell both added, "Yes, please."

Juliet hurried to the archway and had a quick, soft conversation with someone beyond.

She then returned to the living room, perching on her chair, wringing her hands anxiously.

"This is so upsetting. I can't believe she's passed away, and that such a terrible thing happened nearby. Walter, my husband, said we're going to have to review our home security. Do you know if there are any leads?" She stared at them through wide, blue eyes.

Her anxiety was tangible now. Stella could sense it was increasing, and wondered briefly if it was just due to the circumstances of the murder, or if there was another reason for it.

"We're hoping you might be able to help us with possible leads and other information, ma'am," Roth said.

"Me? I—well, I will if I can, but I don't know what help I could be. She was such a lovely person. Gentle. I can't imagine anyone disliking her, never mind—that."

She stared down at the pale Persian rug on the tiles.

At that moment, a genial-looking housemaid brought in a tray of coffee and cookies. With a smile, she served everyone. Stella took her mug appreciatively, breathing in the rich aroma of the brew.

When the housemaid had gone, Roth continued.

"How well did you know Amanda?"

"We met about two months ago. She was new to the neighborhood. My friend Cassidy was the first one to meet her and Cassidy invited her to join our bridge game. We were looking for a fourth player as another friend had moved away, so we were one short. From then on, we saw each other once or twice a week. We used to take turns at people's houses. The last game was actually here."

"What time were your games?"

"We started at ten a.m. We'd play for a couple of hours, then have some wine and a light lunch. It usually wrapped up at about two. It was fun, like a real girls' outing. We had lots of laughs. Gossiped a bit," Juliet admitted, her face lighting up at the memory.

Roth drained the last of his coffee and reached for a second cookie. Stella guessed they were his weak point. Maxwell, on the other hand, had only drunk half his cup and not touched the plate of treats.

"Did Amanda mention anything during the gossip?" Roth then questioned in a gentle voice.

"Like what sort of thing?"

"Any personal issues, any difficulties. Perhaps she was feeling angry, or she'd had a confrontation with somebody?"

Juliet thought, frowning slightly, and then shook her head. "I don't recall anything like that at all. That was what made these mornings such fun. It was always lighthearted. We didn't get into anything deep."

Stella didn't know about the bridge mornings, but she could see that Juliet was nervous about going into any detail. She was naturally a reserved person and was holding herself back. Again, she wondered why. Did she have something to hide? Or was she just one of those introverted people who shut down when questioned by strangers?

"What did you speak about?" Roth asked curiously.

"We chatted about the kids—well, Cassidy's kids as she's the only one who has them so far. And our homes, our yoga lessons, our gym sessions. New shops, new restaurants, and we networked a lot of people who did work in our homes."

"Any specific service providers you both used?"

"I know Amanda ended up using our garden services company. They came to her place twice a week. They're locally owned and very well established."

Roth nodded. Then he exchanged a glance with Maxwell. Maxwell gave the tiniest of shrugs in response. Stella guessed he couldn't think of any more questions. Nor could she.

"Thank you so much for your time. You've been very helpful."

From Roth's tone, Stella couldn't tell if he really meant it or if he also felt they had been subtly stonewalled during this interview.

"Do you think you'll find who did it?" Juliet asked anxiously, as they stood up.

"We will do our best, Mrs. Brand," Roth reassured her as they left.

Stella climbed into the car feeling stumped. She'd hoped that interview would have shed at least a gleam of light on the situation, but all it had done was reinforce the fact that Amanda was a gentle, likeable person with no grudges against anyone.

She wished she'd been able to have some alone time with Juliet. Perhaps a one-on-one chat with another woman would have helped break through her reserve. She guessed a few glasses of wine might have helped, too. Anything to get her to speak more freely.

What else did she think about Juliet? Analyzing the interview carefully, Stella decided that despite her reserve, Juliet was a people pleaser who was highly motivated to comply and do the right thing. That could have been why she was so restrained, not wanting to say anything wrong. Her anxiety levels meant that she'd crumple easily if she was confronted or accused. She was glad that Roth had sensed this, and handled the interview in a sensitive way.

Maxwell's impatient sigh told her he felt frustrated by the lack of progress.

"That wasn't as productive as I'd hoped," Roth agreed grimly. "I hope we get more from the other two friends who were part of this little circle."

But, as they climbed into the car, Roth's phone rang.

He spoke for a minute and Stella saw his body language change. He sat up straight and she felt a prickle of excitement as she heard the tone of his voice sharpen.

"That was the New Haven office on the line. There's been a breakthrough," he said.

"What?" Stella asked, feeling hopeful.

"Police arrested a suspect in the Waterbury stabbing case," Roth said. "The man was caught for speeding and then tried to flee when they pulled him over. They've taken him into custody in Thomaston."

"That's about forty-five minutes from here," Maxwell said. "We can get there tonight still."

"The problem is, we have another important interview," Roth said. "My office has located the previous owners of the Logans' house, who employed the cleaner we've been unable to get hold of. They relocated to Stamford, and are willing to speak to us, but they said it needs to be tonight, if possible."

Stamford was in the opposite direction from Thomaston. Which of these two important angles would take priority? Stella wondered.

With a sigh, Roth made his decision.

"Maxwell, you're the one who's been focused on the drug aspect. Maxwell was part of the team who cracked a series of drug-related killings soon after he joined," Roth explained to Stella. "So you go to Thomaston. Stella and I will head to Stamford."

"Drop me off at the precinct and I'll take a car from there," Maxwell said, sounding enthusiastic.

Stella was glad that Roth had chosen for her to go with him. She couldn't wait to find out more about the person who had worked in close proximity to Amanda ever since her move to Fairfield.

CHAPTER THIRTEEN

It was after nine by the time Stella and Roth arrived at the luxury apartments where the previous owners of the Logans' home now lived. The imposing building was close enough to the ocean for her to hear, as well as smell, the sea.

Roth signed in with the doorman, who directed them across the plushly carpeted lobby to one of the three elevators.

"We're interviewing Mr. and Mrs. Gallagher, who employed Maylin, the previous cleaner. I have no idea what to expect. My office just said they were prepared to speak to us urgently," Roth said, as the elevator made a hushed, speedy ascent to the tenth floor, where the doors opened smoothly.

Stella felt even more expectant. Why the rush? Did they have something important to share with the FBI?

They strode over more thick carpet to apartment 1001. Roth pressed the bell and a moment later, the door opened.

A slim woman with an immaculately coiffed, blue-white bob stood facing them. She looked to be in her early seventies. She was wearing a gorgeous green and gold coat, and she gave a welcoming smile.

"Good evening. I'm Lara Gallagher."

"FBI Special Agents Roth and Fall," Roth introduced them politely.

"Come in, Officers, please. Join us in the living room. Harold, the FBI is here to find out what we can tell them about this terrible killing."

Chattily, Mrs. Gallagher led the way through a side door into a sumptuously furnished room, with plush sofas, wingback chairs, and finely crafted tables with delicate legs.

Mr. Gallagher was seated in one of the wingback chairs, reading a book. He hastily closed it and scrambled stiffly to his feet to welcome them. Having shaken their hands, he sat down again, casting a longing glance at his book.

"Thank you for seeing us so promptly. We won't take much of your time," Roth said as they all took a seat. Perching on the chair next to him, Stella picked up a hint of a question in the words.

"We're leaving for vacation tomorrow. We're going to Sydney for my granddaughter's wedding, so we'll be very busy packing and making all our last-minute preparations. That's why I asked you to come by tonight. I wanted to try and help. That house was our home for forty years. I cannot believe such a dreadful crime took place there," Mrs. Gallagher said.

Stella felt disappointed that the reason for the rush had been a planned vacation, and nothing more serious.

"You employed the cleaner, Maylin, who worked for the Logans until yesterday," Roth said, getting straight to the point of the visit. "Our office hasn't been able to contact her, and the cell number Craig Logan gave us is no longer operational. Do you have any alternative numbers for her, or any of her friends and relatives?"

Stella held her breath. She hoped that these people would have the information they needed to track her down.

But Lara shook her head. "No, I don't," she said sadly.

As Roth was drawing a breath to ask another question, Lara spoke again.

"There's nothing sinister about it. I just don't have any details as yet. She's not contactable right now because she's gone back home permanently. She lives in Santa Rosa de Copan, in Honduras."

"I see," Roth said, clearly reserving judgment. "What was she like as a person? How long did she work for you?"

Lara's face warmed. "Maylin was a gem. An absolute gem! She started working for us when we moved into Begonia Drive, when our two children were still young. She really was part of the family and lived in with us during the week for years. What an incredible person. We wanted her to carry on working for us when we downscaled, but she decided to retire. All her family are back home and she wanted to spend time with her new grandchild when he was born."

Stella felt frustrated. In terms of criminal profiles, the treasured, and somewhat elderly, family retainer was about as far from a prime suspect as could be.

"So she stayed on to look after the house for a while?" Roth asked.

"That's right. We moved out in April and got the home nicely fixed up before we put it on the market. She looked after it during that time and kept it sparkling. It sold very fast, and then she worked for the new owners mornings only, while they settled in."

"Did you keep in touch with her during that time?" Stella asked. It sounded as if they had been good enough friends to stay in contact.

"Of course. We spoke every couple of weeks," Mrs. Gallagher said. "We were buying her ticket back to Honduras so we had to keep up to date with her plans."

"Exactly," Mr. Gallagher said suddenly, causing Stella to turn in his direction in surprise. "We made sure to look after her."

With that, as if he'd now said what he had to, he picked up his book again.

"And she flew yesterday?" Roth said.

"That's right. Her grandson was born a few days ago so I believe she then gave immediate notice and asked the family to find someone else urgently. She worked her last morning yesterday and we booked her on the seven p.m. flight back home," Mrs. Gallagher said with a smile.

Even though this was not sounding like their suspect, Stella wondered if perhaps the maid knew something important.

"Did Maylin ever speak to you about the Logans? Did she mention anything unusual about her new employers?" Stella asked. She saw Roth give a nod of approval at this question.

"Let me think, let me think," Mrs. Gallagher mused. "Yes. There was something she mentioned a couple of days ago that made me think things were not perfect. It troubled me at the time, but now, I can't recall exactly what it was." She sighed.

Stella wished that Mrs. Gallagher had taken this more seriously and discussed it in more detail. It could provide the lead they needed.

"How can we get hold of Maylin?" Roth asked.

"She said she'd contact us as soon as she set up her new phone. That could be any minute." Mrs. Gallagher smiled hopefully. "Or it might only be tomorrow."

"Please can you urgently pass the number on to us when you have it?" Roth asked.

"Of course. We're leaving late afternoon tomorrow. I'm sure she'll call before then."

"Thank you for your time." Roth stood up.

Mr. Gallagher hastily put down his book. "Thank you, Officers," he barked.

They headed out.

Stella felt disappointed as she left the ornately decorated apartment. She'd hoped for more information, and for the cleaner to be a strong suspect. Worse still, the tantalizing issue Maylin had mentioned was still unclear.

Going down in the elevator, Roth checked his phone and his face tightened in disappointment.

"Bad news from Maxwell," he said, sounding grimly resigned.

"What happened?" Stella asked, feeling even more worried.

"The suspect they arrested in Thomaston has confessed to the Waterbury murder, after being confronted with the evidence. But he has a solid alibi for the night of the Logan killing. He was holed up in a motel near Thomaston with a friend. Phone records confirm it. So he's not our man. It rules out the serial aspect of the crime."

"What does that mean for us?" Stella asked.

"Normally we would step away at this point, but given the circumstances of this case, the level of violence, and the extreme pressure from the town council and the authorities higher up, I'm going to make the call for us to stay involved for longer. We need to solve it," he emphasized, sounding determined.

Stella felt relieved by his decision. She couldn't imagine stepping away from the case now, when the frustrating mystery of Amanda's death had started to consume her.

They climbed into the car.

"What's our plan now?" she asked as they headed onto the highway.

"We start again first thing tomorrow, focusing on Amanda's friends and contacts. We still have two more of her closest friends to interview."

"I hope they're more talkative than the first one was," Stella volunteered.

"They surely couldn't be less talkative than Juliet, so let's stay positive," Roth agreed. "I'm going to go back to New Haven and review the case notes, consult with my team, see if there's anything we missed. They've already booked you into a hotel in Fairfield for the night, so I'll drop you off there and pick you up in the morning at eight. If there's anything you need, any extra clothing, bags, or personal items, buy them and keep the slip. You'll be refunded as part of the investigation expenses."

Roth's brief, sympathetic smile showed Stella he'd noticed the absence of any travel bags or personal possessions.

She wished she could go back to New Haven with Roth and review the notes. It felt frustrating to step away from an unsolved case for the night, especially when the team was under so much pressure to find the killer.

But perhaps thinking about the interviews they'd done so far, in the quiet of the hotel room, would give her some fresh and important insights on the case.

*

Stella opened her eyes, feeling disoriented in the strange hotel room. She couldn't hear the faint hum of the AC, or the swishing sounds of traffic outside. The room seemed larger than she remembered, and the pink edge of dawn was only just brightening the curtains.

She glanced to the side and screamed.

There it was. The bloodied body that she'd never forgotten. The sight was etched in her memory and imprinted on her subconscious. She'd always be screaming, deep inside, at the horror of seeing her dead fiancé.

Except it wasn't. She yelled louder as she saw the body lying next to her belonged to Amanda. The slashes and smears of blood looked like an outrage on her pale, flawless skin.

"You did this! It's your fault! You caused this and now nothing can fix it. It's broken forever. Forever!"

Stella recognized that berating voice only too well. The words and tone were seared into her memory, and no matter how hard she tried to fight them, they always refused to leave.

She raised her eyes from the terrible sight of the corpse and stared into the implacable gaze of her mother.

And then she sat up, jerking out of her nightmare with a cry, breathing hard, staring into the darkness as the specter of the dream finally subsided.

What time was it? she wondered. She didn't think she could go back to sleep after that. Her skin was still prickling with terror and dread. She'd fallen asleep stressing over the case and her subconscious must have picked up on the last murder she'd been personally caught up in.

Checking her phone, Stella was thankful to see that it was six-thirty a.m. This was the time she usually woke at Quantico. On a normal day she'd spend half an hour in the gym before grabbing a quick breakfast and then starting the long, arduous day of study, practical experience, and physical training.

Who knew what today would bring.

At that moment, her phone rang. Thinking it would be Roth, she grabbed it off the charger, then was delighted to see that it was her best friend, Rebecca, on the line.

Rebecca had gone to school with her in the Midwest. They'd known each other since they were twelve. Now she was married and living in New Brunswick. Her home had provided a safe retreat for Stella after the ordeal of her fiancé's murder.

Since Stella had been at the academy, they had spoken every few days, and early mornings were their prearranged time. Especially after her nightmare, she was comforted to be able to have a quick chat with her friend.

"Are you getting ready for an obstacle course or a criminal law class today?" Rebecca asked.

Stella could imagine her in her tiny kitchen, her red hair swinging over her face as she multitasked—feeding the cat, putting on coffee, tackling a load of washing.

Today, Stella was multitasking, too. Switching her phone to speaker, she sprung out of bed, getting changed into one of the new T-shirts she'd bought yesterday at the hotel's kiosk, together with a toothbrush and other basic toiletry items.

"You won't believe this. I'm in Fairfield, helping the FBI with a case. Clem organized it. The academy allowed me to take part."

As Stella spoke, she remembered with a chill what would await her when she got back. Carrie had laid a formal complaint. Today, Marc would be investigating it.

Quickly, she put that chilling thought aside as Rebecca's admiring "Wow" resounded down the line.

"Girlfriend! That's amazing. Your first case already. Why did they call you in?"

"It's a stabbing," Stella confessed, hearing Rebecca's indrawn breath as she instantly understood the parallels in the case, and why Clem had thought she could help.

"Are you coping okay with that?" were her friend's first words. Stella felt grateful for the support.

"Better than I thought I would," she was glad to explain.

"And the killer? Do you know who he or she is?"

"All the leads so far have fizzled out."

"Husband? Isn't it always the husband? That's what you told me," Rebecca suggested.

"He has an alibi. We're interviewing more of her close friends today. They were fairly new in town. It doesn't seem to be a random break-in but the weird thing is she was liked by everyone. So far, nobody's said a bad word."

Rebecca snorted.

"Don't they always warn people not to speak ill of the dead? I'm sure you need to get beyond that sticking point and find someone who'll tell the truth. Nobody's perfect! And nobody's liked by everyone in my experience. Maybe there is that one person who hated her, or who she betrayed."

"I hope we can uncover something like that," Stella said, thinking again of Juliet, and how much she hadn't said. How she wished she'd had some alone time with her.

"Well, I'd better let you run. Let's catch up once you have more time. I hope it goes well and remember my advice, as a social media expert, nobody is perfect or blameless!"

She disconnected, laughing.

As Stella finished getting ready, packing the few belongings she'd bought into the small carrier bag the hotel had provided, she thought about Rebecca's words.

Nobody was perfect and nobody was an angel, but so far, Amanda had been portrayed that way.

Hopefully, today's interviews would uncover the real truth.

CHAPTER FOURTEEN

Roth pulled up outside the hotel at exactly eight a.m. and Stella climbed into the back, stashing her carrier bag under the seat.

She thought Roth looked disheveled, as if he were a few hours short on sleep. In contrast, Maxwell, in the passenger seat, looked fresh, bright-eyed, and well rested. Stella guessed wryly this was more a matter of the men's age difference than their actual hours slept. For someone pushing fifty, working into the small hours on a high-pressure case would take more of a toll.

"Our next interviewee is waiting for us. She lives a couple of miles away from Amanda, and her name is Eleanor Lane. Fall, remember I need you to keep quiet, listen, and watch how things are done." He glanced over his shoulder to frown at her. "And if you think of any questions, make sure you word them appropriately. If you're not sure, take us aside and ask. I don't want any surprises during any of these interviews. Naked or otherwise," he said firmly.

"I promise I will do that," Stella said, but inwardly she couldn't help wondering whether a sudden, unexpected question might have the shock value needed to get results.

She hoped that Eleanor would be a better source of information than Juliet. Perhaps she might have been closer to Amanda. Among four friends, there were going to be stronger alliances. Perhaps Amanda had shared confidences with one of the women that she hadn't with the others. She'd have to keep aware of the dynamic, Stella told herself.

Asking the right question at the right time might just be the key to cracking this case open.

In terms of the neighborhood, Stella was expecting Eleanor's home to be more of the same, and she wasn't wrong, even though she couldn't help hoping that they might find a quirky, purple-painted cottage among the ranks of stately homes. Not a bit of it. This home was a carbon copy of the last, situated even closer to the sea, and when they walked up the garden path and knocked on the door, Stella felt a weird sense of déjà vu as it opened.

Eleanor, standing in the doorway, was as well-groomed as Juliet, only more colorful. Her short, blonde hair was held back by a bright scarf and she wore a rainbow-colored top. Stella thought she looked a little younger and was probably in her mid-twenties.

"Good morning, Officers," she said. She sighed. "As good as it can be. I am hellishly devastated by all of this. Have you worked out what happened yet?"

"Good to meet you, ma'am, and thank you for your time. We're hoping you can provide some insights," Roth said politely.

"Come in, please. I've been sitting in the sun on the back porch, which has a sea view. Shall we speak there?"

She led them through the house to a back porch which was bathed in bright morning sunshine and overlooked a large garden. Beyond, in the distance, was the glimmering ocean.

"You want coffee? Water? Anything?"

"We're fine, thank you," Roth said, taking a seat on one of the plushly upholstered cane chairs.

"What do you want to know?" Eleanor perched on a swing seat, rocking back and forth as she regarded them.

"We need as much background on Amanda as you can possibly provide. We understand you got together for bridge?" Roth said.

"That's correct. The other girls and I had been playing for about a year. Well, that's when I was invited to join. We moved to the area for my husband's work. I think a lot of us are like that," she said with what impressed Stella as self-deprecating honesty. "Hubby gets a promo and then here we are."

Stella felt encouraged. Eleanor seemed more outspoken than Juliet had been. She hoped this trend would continue when the topic moved to Amanda herself.

"When did you meet Amanda?" Roth asked.

"Cassidy met her and invited her to play," Eleanor said with a slight smile, which Stella realized confirmed what Juliet had said. Eleanor's smile then faded and she grimaced. "It's horrible to think we had such fun. This has hit us hard. It still seems impossible."

"What were your sessions like?" Maxwell asked.

Stella guessed he was confirming Juliet's version. While he checked the logistical side, she wanted to focus more on the interactions within the group.

"We started with a game, which lasted a couple of hours. We'd play a few rounds."

"Who partnered with Amanda?" Stella asked. She hoped she wouldn't get a warning glance for this innocent question, but wanted to know if it signaled any closer relationships within the group.

To her surprise, Eleanor looked briefly confused by the question.

"We used to alternate," Eleanor then explained. "We didn't have permanent partners. We'd draw names at the start of the game. I think it was a good idea as it helped keep it fair and friendly. And it was very friendly."

Something about that struck a discordant note with Stella. Why had it piqued her instincts? she wondered. However, she felt too immersed in the moment to pull herself out of it. In the meantime she needed to concentrate on Eleanor.

"So you played for a couple of hours?" Roth echoed.

"Then we had wine, lunch, and chat. It was more about the chat, really. The fun. It was always so lighthearted. We'd wrap up just before two, when Cassidy's kids came home from school."

Now Stella felt frustration rising again. This was going the same way as Juliet's interview had. Eleanor was glossing over the sessions rather than providing any important details. Well, perhaps she could find out more.

"What did you discuss during your chats?" she asked.

Eleanor sighed. "You know what they say? Small minds discuss people, big minds discuss ideas? I'm afraid we were firmly in the small minds category. We chatted about family, neighbors, our gym and yoga classes. We networked a lot on service providers. Pool companies, garden services, landscapers."

More of the same, Stella thought. Eleanor was describing the type of conversation you'd have in a grocery store line, not in a get-together of close friends. Everyone had fears, worries, and dreams. Everyone needed someone to share them with. She thought of her conversation with Rebecca earlier that morning. That was what a chat between friends should be like.

"Did Amanda ever mention personal issues? Ever ask about anything that was bothering her, or look for emotional advice? Extra security, anything like that?" Roth said.

"No. I've been racking my brains about it, as I also feel that we maybe missed something. That she was crying for help and we weren't listening. But there was nothing." She stared into the distance with a considering expression. "If I'm honest, though, I would say she was more closed than average. She didn't share much personal stuff."

Stella sensed that this last statement was more authentic than anything else Eleanor had said.

They sat another minute. She guessed Roth was seeking another angle to persuade Eleanor to open up and say something more, but he couldn't think of one. And nor could she. According to Eleanor's account, these games had been simple socializing, and she wasn't budging from her version.

"Thank you so much for your time. You've been very helpful," Roth said.

They stood up and walked out.

The car was pleasantly warm from having been parked in the sun. They climbed in, and Roth said, "Well, what did you think of that?"

"I think they are holding something back," Maxwell said. "There's a notable lack of information coming from them."

"I can't see four women getting together every week and not getting close," Stella agreed. "Especially with the lives they led, and the fact they had wine at lunch. Of course they'd end up sharing personal information and getting involved in absolutely everything."

"Exactly," Roth said.

"There's something else as well. Something that's bothering me. I can't put my finger on it, though. If I do think of it, you won't mind if I ask a sudden question?" Stella asked, frustrated by the information that seemed to be eluding her, tauntingly just unable to be grasped.

"At this stage, I won't mind if you ask them all if they played nude bridge," Roth said. She thought he was only half joking, but something in his statement gave her more of a clue. Her mind latched onto it.

"In fact," Roth added, "you two can run the next interview with Cassidy Cooper. We need a change of pace. I'm tired of asking the same questions and getting the same replies. Perhaps one of you can break through and get something different."

Stella exchanged a glance with Maxwell. She could see Maxwell was pleased to be getting a chance to be more active, but definitely resentful of doing so with Stella.

Too bad, she thought. Now that Roth had handed them both the job, she planned to do whatever she could to find out more.

So, who was Eleanor? she summarized to herself as they drove.

Eleanor was more gregarious than Juliet. She was more impulsive. Naturally a greater extrovert. Stella had the sense she'd be a better liar and more able to think on her feet. Given that thought, she'd also be more unpredictable if she was pushed out of her comfort zone.

She hoped her mental notes might be of some use at some future stage.

"Here's our next home. Cassidy Cooper." With a sigh, Roth pulled up outside a mansion that was, if anything, larger than the others. Otherwise it was from the same mold. Stella noted a jungle gym and swing under the oak tree, and remembered the others had said Cassidy had children.

Cassidy herself was outside in the garden, holding an armful of blooms. When she saw the detectives, she turned and hurried to them.

"Good morning, Officers. Please, come inside. I'm so glad to see you. I hope you are going to be able to provide answers for us, as we're all traumatized."

Cassidy was the prettiest of all the women. She was tall, model-slim, and had burnished blond hair that cascaded over her shoulders. Her tank top showed off toned, tanned arms, although as she went inside, she slipped a cashmere jacket on. She paused in the hallway, where the walls were lined with framed mirrors and oil paintings, to place the flowers in a large porcelain vase.

Then they were ushered into the immaculate living room. Stella stared around in awe. Clearly, Cassidy had either traveled widely or had sourced décor items from other countries. She recognized Venetian vases, Persian rugs, Italian tapestries.

"My husband is an art dealer. He runs an art and antiques supply business," Cassidy explained, seeing Stella's admiring gaze.

Stella seated herself on a lime green armchair. Maxwell, scowling, sat on a cream one opposite. Roth perched on a wooden antique rocking chair, and Cassidy stood by the window.

"Can I bring you any refreshments?" she asked in caring tones.

"We're good, thanks." This time it was Maxwell's turn to decline the offer. Only then did Cassidy perch herself on the cushioned love seat.

As she laced her fingers over her slender knees, Stella noticed her immaculate manicure, and the gold bracelet on her wrist which was studded with green and blue gems. Stella guessed they were emeralds and sapphires.

"Tell me about your friendship with Amanda," Maxwell invited.

Cassidy drew a breath.

"I met her in town one day. We bumped into each other at a furniture shop. She was new in town, and we got talking as we browsed. We were looking out for a fourth in our bridge game and I was thrilled to find a new player. Not to mention having another friend in our little circle."

"When did you meet?"

"I can check in my diary." Cassidy pursed her lips thoughtfully. "No, no, I don't need to. I remember it was the second Monday in August, because it was my son's birthday the next Monday."

"How did the mornings play out?"

"We'd play a couple of hours of bridge. Then we'd have lunch and chat."

"What did Amanda tell you about herself?"

Cassidy sighed. "She wasn't that forthcoming. Quite a private person, I think. She obviously talked a lot about her home, her husband's new job, the crazy hours he was working. It meant we could help her with a lot of information on sourcing decorators, garden services and the like. They were limited by his working hours on what they could do together."

"Did your husbands ever get together with you ladies?" Maxwell then tried.

"No, unfortunately one of the reasons we need a local circle is that our husbands work very long and unsocial hours. One of the common factors is how much time they spend at the office, or traveling. Obviously when they are home, we have really good quality time. But when they are not, at least we all have friends who understand this," Cassidy admitted.

"Did Amanda have other friends locally? Maybe she spoke to you about people she met, people she was staying in touch with from her previous area?"

"She definitely mentioned that from time to time. But the problem was that it was all so ordinary that I can't remember the details. It wasn't like I wasn't listening to her. Of course I was. But nothing seemed important enough to worry about, if you understand." Cassidy spread her hands. "If there had been any issues or conflict—well, of course we would have helped her with it in a flash. But I guess she was too new here. She was still finding her feet and making friends. I do remember how lighthearted all our get-togethers were. It was a chance to just laugh and gossip and have fun."

If Stella heard the word "lighthearted" one more time, she decided—well, she decided she was going to start wondering if they'd collaborated on their versions. Certainly, so far, they might as well have interviewed one of the women three times, than interview three of them once each.

Suddenly, in a flash of insight, Roth's earlier comment came back to her and the niggling inconsistency she'd sensed became more concrete. Finally, she understood what it was. She knew she had a single chance, one chance only, to test her theory and catch Cassidy out.

How could she do it? Stella thought furiously.

CHAPTER FIFTEEN

Stella stared at Cassidy, assessing her. She was intelligent, quick-minded, and could think on her feet. She used her charm as a weapon. Stella had the feeling that her persona was so much a part of her that she wouldn't give it up, no matter what.

There was also an air of superiority about her.

Quickly, Stella assessed how she might be able to work with these qualities.

"I know very little about bridge," she said with a laugh. "Is it really so fascinating that you played it every week?"

"Oh, yes," Cassidy stated confidently. "It's a very addictive game."

"Did you always have the same partners?" Stella asked, wondering if she would confirm the facts Eleanor had given.

Cassidy gave a bright, confident smile. "We drew names at the start of each session. It kept it fairer. We were all happy to play with whoever we drew."

Stella suppressed the sudden, strong vision she had of Eleanor calling Cassidy urgently as soon as they'd left, and telling her to say this. The original question had taken Eleanor by surprise. Now, Cassidy was saying something virtually identical.

Did they not want to disclose who'd been Amanda's regular partner or was there another, very different, reason? Perhaps the next question would reveal more, Stella hoped.

"What kind of bridge did you play?" she asked.

Cassidy looked at her, as surprised as Eleanor had been, as if she hadn't expected such a question.

"Did you play rubber bridge or sterling bridge?" Stella asked. "Those are the only two types I've heard of. There might be others I don't know about."

Cassidy smiled. "Sterling, most times," she said.

Maxwell gave her a despairing glance as if he'd hoped for a question that would shed more light. Since she didn't have one, Stella simply sat back in her chair and waited for him to conclude the interview.

“Thank you so much for your time,” he said. “We may need to follow up with more questions in the next day or two.”

“I’m available, any time. I will literally drop whatever I’m doing to help you guys,” Cassidy said.

It was impossible not to be spellbound by her beauty and charm.

They got up and walked out. Returning to the car, the men were silent. Stella was thinking hard.

They climbed inside.

“Okay. What other leads do we have?” Roth asked, sounding exasperated. “That was the most routine and unhelpful set of interviews I’ve had in years. We need to move on. None of these ladies know anything that can help us.”

Stella cleared her throat. “Actually, I think they do,” she said.

Maxwell turned around to scowl at her disbelievingly. “And you have decided this how?”

“Let’s drive. She’s watching us from the front door. I’ll tell you when we’re out of sight,” Stella warned.

Roth started the car and headed around the corner. He drove a few hundred yards, turned left, drove another minute, and then pulled into the parking lot of a hair and beauty salon.

“What information did you pick up?” He turned to stare at her. There was challenge in his gaze.

“They’re all lying,” Stella told him.

“All?” Maxwell asked incredulously. “Why do you say that?”

“There’s no style of bridge called sterling. I made it up,” Stella said. “The three most common styles of bridge are rubber, duplicate, and Chicago.”

There was an astounded silence in the car. It lasted a few heartbeats. Then Maxwell let out an amazed guffaw.

“You serious?” he said.

“I’m serious,” Stella confirmed.

“That’s downright brilliant.” Roth sounded equal parts amused and impressed. “I didn’t suspect it for a moment. No such thing as sterling bridge? She sounded as if she was an authority on it.”

“I led her into the question, setting myself up as someone who knew nothing so she wouldn’t suspect,” Stella said, feeling a surge of pride at Roth’s praise. Finally, she was providing some real value to the team. “I doubt they know how to play at all. This whole bridge story didn’t sound legitimate from the get-go. I had a university lecturer who was a passionate bridge player and I picked up a bit about it. I was able to recall some facts in the car on the way to Cassidy's, and I realized that two hours is on the short side, especially for a regular game. They're usually three or more hours. Given that, I thought I'd test the entire premise."

"Well!" Maxwell said.

"Okay. Are you certain about this? If so it gives us a starting point. If they were lying, they lied for a reason and that means they don't want us to know what they were really doing during these lighthearted get-togethers," Roth said.

Stella was briefly amused by the fact that word had clearly irked Roth as much as it had her.

"I'm certain. There is no such thing as sterling bridge," she reiterated.

"So what do we do now?" Roth asked thoughtfully.

"Should we not find out where they were on the night of the murder?" Stella said, feeling hopeful that they at last had a lead. "Can we pull their phone records? Their social media might even help us."

But, to her surprise, Roth raised a warning hand.

"No. We can't do any of that."

"Why not?" Stella asked.

"Because, right now, they think they got away with this, that they're in the clear and we don't know a thing. There's a lot to be said for observing unsuspecting individuals, and if you take one thing away from your time with us, let it be that. You get far, far more from them that way, than if we start accusing them and overtly digging into their lives."

"I understand," Stella said, feeling impressed with his wisdom. She was learning so much on this case. Now she could see this was the better course of action.

"Okay. This is our plan. Maxwell, we never confirmed that Amanda was really at that yoga class. The instructor didn't answer your call, so head over there, find if it's true, and see what the class was all about."

"Will do," Maxwell said.

"I'm going to pull her phone records and texts, see who she contacted and if anything was said or organized."

Stella waited to hear what she would be tasked with.

"Fall, I want you to pick one of the three women we interviewed today and shadow her for the rest of the day. Make sure you remain unnoticed. I want to know where she goes, whether she does anything suspicious—and if she meets up with either of the other two."

"I'll start with Cassidy," Stella said.

"Good. Let's drive to New Haven and you can take a car," Roth said.

Stella felt unreasonably excited. This was her first ever undercover assignment. And Roth was driving, not to the local police precinct, but to the FBI office in New Haven.

It was a longer drive, not just a couple of minutes, and Stella passed the time by thinking about how she would shadow Cassidy. All the women had seemed intelligent and aware. Perhaps that was one of the reasons why their naïve comments had made the team suspicious, as the agents had expected more perceptive insights. She'd have to make very sure to stay out of sight, and not alert her that she was being followed.

"I will go in and report back on our decision to keep investigating this case as a result of governmental pressure. But we'll get your car sorted first so you can get going," Roth said.

*

Forty minutes later, Stella headed out of the New Haven office behind the wheel of a nondescript white Ford. It was her first ever unmarked, and her first ever surveillance assignment. She had to admit, it felt good to be away from the two men and operating on her own. Thinking of the challenges ahead, she stopped at a nearby convenience store. Rushing in, she purchased a pair of shades and a baseball cap to help with her cover.

As she pocketed the slip and climbed back in the car, she warned herself not to let her excitement get in the way of doing her job properly. The one thing that would impress Roth, and perhaps even Maxwell, was if she got results. She'd had tuition hours on surveillance at the academy and they were fresh in her mind.

She turned into the street where Cassidy lived, stopping the car when she was one house away from her home. She pulled onto the verge and watched the driveway. Would Cassidy go out anywhere?

Stella had worried about being conspicuous in this quiet neighborhood populated by so many non-working wives, but she was relieved that there was a lot of activity in the area. She guessed there was a kindergarten school close by, because cars were coming and going, driven by young women and with small children belted into the back seat. Not luxury cars, either, but cars similar to her Ford. She guessed that many residents in the area used au pairs.

There she was. Stella drew in a breath as she saw Cassidy drive out behind the wheel of a Volvo station wagon.

She turned in the opposite direction from Stella.

Was she going to pick up children? She seemed very smartly dressed, Stella thought. But maybe that was just the way she was. Her hair was flawlessly done, and she was wearing bright lipstick. Stella recalled that when they had visited, her lipstick had been more toned down, perhaps due to the solemnity of their visit. Now, it matched the cerise tones in the gorgeous floral jacket she wore.

She pulled away in pursuit, and as she passed by the house, she realized she could, in fact, rule one possibility out. In the garden, two blond children were playing on the jungle gym, supervised by a young woman in her early twenties.

So the kids were home and being looked after by the au pair, and that meant Cassidy was heading out somewhere different than the school pick-up.

Stella accelerated down the street, catching a glimpse of the silver Volvo as it turned left. A quick left turn and she had caught up with it, enough to keep the car in view, at any rate. She didn't want to get too close to it and risk being spotted.

Cassidy made another turn onto the main road and sped down it. Stella turned, too. She looked to be heading into town. Where was she going?

Ahead, a light turned yellow. The Volvo's brake lights flashed, and Stella slowed.

But then, impatiently, Cassidy accelerated through the light as it turned red, powering the car around another left-hand turn.

Stella swore, clutching the steering wheel with hands that were damp with tension. She couldn't follow, and now, thanks to the rows of buildings, she couldn't see where Cassidy had gone.

Could she have done that better? Stella wondered, feeling filled with self-blame. She decided she could, and should, have. She'd made a rookie error by being too far behind when approaching a light. That was the time to close up the distance and be prepared for a sudden decision, Stella thought, trying to swallow down her disappointment.

The light changed again and Stella waited for the oncoming traffic to pass before she too took the left turn at last.

The street ahead was empty and there was no sign of Cassidy or the Volvo. She could have gone anywhere, and Stella reluctantly admitted she wouldn't catch her now. Too much time had passed.

This surveillance was definitely easier in theory. She'd aced her classes in it, she remembered resentfully. Now, in her very first real case, she'd messed up.

Still, she wasn't going to give up. Not when there were other suspects waiting for their turn.

Stella decided that if Cassidy had disappeared, she was going to follow Juliet. Rerouting her satnav, she turned in the direction of Juliet's home.

At that moment, her phone rang.

It was Maxwell.

"How's things going there?" he asked.

Stella sighed. "Frustrating. I followed Cassidy into town. She looked dressed to the nines. But I lost her at a light."

If she'd expected sympathy, it wasn't forthcoming.

"Didn't you do classes on that at the academy?" Maxwell asked, sounding accusing. "You should watch out for getting too far behind next time."

Stella felt her cheeks burn with the well-deserved criticism.

"I'm arriving at Juliet's house now. Her car's outside the garage so it looks as if she might be heading out somewhere at some stage. This time I'm going to be sharper," she promised.

"I hope you find something. Because I have nothing. The yoga class was a dead end." Maxwell also sounded frustrated.

"Why's that?"

"It was a one-on-one class. Private tuition from the instructor who's a middle-aged woman, and very professional. It was very clear that this was all about yoga. She's extremely busy, she says, and it looked to be that way. I had to wait an hour for a five-minute gap in between two of her clients. Then she told me that Amanda was pleasant, quiet, and they didn't discuss anything outside of yoga. She says she seldom does, because she seldom has time. It's a quick chitchat and then a forty-five-minute session. For which she charges a fortune." Maxwell sounded both impressed and disapproving.

"Are we going to get a break on this? How much longer will Roth keep us on the case, do you know?" Stella asked, feeling worried.

"I have no idea. I'm going to head back and meet up with him, see if there's any progress on his side," Maxwell told her.

"I'll stay here and see if Juliet goes out at all." At that moment, Stella saw the front door open. "Hey! I have something happening here. I'd better go."

Quickly, she disconnected. She wasn't going to lose another tail. The last failure was still scorching her. She was determined to follow Juliet at all costs. She was going to find out where she went.

CHAPTER SIXTEEN

Juliet was dressed smartly, too, Stella noticed, as the slim woman climbed into her black BMW. Was that significant? Through narrowed eyes, Stella watched her leave her gate. She counted down a few seconds and then pulled casually away.

Immediately, she saw that Juliet was a less aware driver than Cassidy had been. It was interesting how you could pick up on this in a moment when following someone. Cassidy had been fast, impatient, and decisive. Juliet was meandering all over the road. A couple of times, she veered over the center line before hastily correcting herself. Was she multitasking? Stella wondered, as an approaching motorist flashed his lights angrily and honked his horn at her. Was Juliet putting on lipstick or maybe reading a text?

At any rate, this was lucky for her, because it meant she wouldn't be paying attention to anyone who might be following.

She was heading into town also. Stella followed her closely, staying alert for any lights changing ahead and any signs Juliet might go ahead with the same impatient left turn.

She didn't. She made a right turn without indicating, then slowed, and then overshot an empty parking spot. Quickly, she reversed and pulled in.

The spot was close to a restaurant that looked to be emptying out after breakfast. Checking the time, Stella saw it was nearly eleven a.m. Maybe this was just a coffee meet-up with a friend.

Sweat prickled Stella's brow as she accelerated along the street, keeping an eye out for an open parking spot. The logistics of surveillance were way more stressful than she'd expected. There was a spot. Grateful for her compact unmarked, Stella wedged the car speedily into it and scrambled out, grabbing the baseball cap to cover her dark hair so that she wouldn't be recognizable at a glance.

Where was Juliet? She didn't seem to be at the restaurant's front desk, waiting to be seated. Had she gone directly inside to join someone? Feeling frantic, Stella scanned the faces.

Then, the honk of a horn attracted her attention in a different direction. She glanced at the road and drew in a quick breath.

Juliet was crossing the road, and had stepped out in front of an annoyed-looking cab driver. With an apologetic wave to the angry man, she rushed across.

Watching her, grateful that she was wearing a black-and-white patterned jacket that stood out, Stella saw her head into a building on the other side. The four-story building was a hotel.

Was this a coffee date, but in a different place? Yet again, Stella felt on the back foot as she waited for a gap in the suddenly worsening traffic, so that she, too, could rush across the road. She wished she had more experience in doing this. It was a critical part of the investigation and she didn't feel she was nearly on top of this important skill.

For a start, she wasn't sure what to do now. Should she check in with Roth and ask what the next step should be?

Stella decided to take a look inside the hotel first and confirm where Juliet was. Roth might need that information to make his decisions.

Besides, her instincts were telling her there was something very odd about this. The restaurant, with a few empty tables and its pretty outdoor seating, looked like the ideal meet-up point, so why go into the hotel?

Stella walked inside, hoping she could take the situation in at a glance.

There was a reception desk at the far side of the lobby, but at this moment there was nobody in attendance there, and the door behind the reception area stood ajar. To the right was a small lounge with a couple of unoccupied tables. And to the left was an annex where an elevator was located. As Stella watched, surprised, Juliet stepped into the elevator and the doors closed behind her.

Sidling closer, Stella took a look at the floor numbers. Where was the elevator stopping?

It stopped on the third floor. As soon as she saw the number light up and stay lit, Stella dived for the stairs. Pushing open the door, she powered up the flights, arriving breathlessly at floor three a minute later.

The hallway was thickly carpeted and quiet. Doors stretched to the left and right. Rooms one to four were to the left. Five to eight were to the right. Turning right, Stella rounded the corner. There was no sign of anyone. All the way at the end of the corridor was a glass door that led into a small gym, equipped with an exercise bicycle, a treadmill, a rowing machine, and a few shiny-looking weights.

The gym was empty. Standing in there, Stella called Roth.

"There's something strange going on here," she said in a low voice.

"What? Where are you?" he replied sharply.

"I'm in a mid-priced hotel opposite a restaurant on the main street in town. Juliet walked in and now she's up here, on the third floor, in one of the rooms."

"Do you know which room?" Roth's voice was sharp.

"I don't. I was just in time to see her going up in the elevator. By the time I followed, she'd gone."

"That might be significant," Roth mused. "It might also be unrelated. We'll have to wait and see. It's all we've got so far. I pulled Amanda's calls for the last six months, and there's nothing unremarkable there. No signs of any harassment. There were routine messages to friends and family back home, and quite a few calls to various stores and service providers. They all check out."

"What should I do now?" Stella asked.

"I'm waiting for one final list to come in and then I'll leave and join you there. Where's this hotel? Send me the name and I'll come through as soon as I can. Meanwhile, wait outside the building. If she leaves, call me and follow her. And be discreet. Make sure she doesn't notice you."

He disconnected, leaving Stella wishing he'd stayed on the line a minute longer.

She'd been about to suggest that she wait here, on the third floor, to see if she could find out which room Juliet was in. But perhaps she could do that anyway.

"Shouldn't I stay up here instead?" she said into the dead phone. "Just in case I'm able to see or hear anything? Hello, Roth, are you there? Hello?"

"Well, I guess I'll wait here anyway," Stella said to herself. At least she could now use the excuse that she thought she'd told Roth. Right now, this really did seem like an important lead. And there was something so weird about it.

There was really only one reason for a well-dressed woman to detour into a mid-priced hotel during the day, which was that the woman was having an affair.

It just didn't seem to fit in with Juliet's life. Who was the affair with? Why on earth were they meeting in such a place?

She sent the address to Roth and then waited, pacing up and down the corridor, listening for any sounds of a door opening, or for anyone arriving who might ask her what she was doing here. It would be difficult to explain her presence to a cleaner or chambermaid. Stella decided if she saw anyone like that, she'd bolt for the gym.

The other problem was that the hotel was shaped like a U, with the elevator at the halfway point. Because of the bends in the corridor, she couldn't see all the doors at once. She wished she had an idea which direction Juliet had gone.

She walked up and down, her footsteps soundless on the carpet.

And then, as she was passing by door number two for what seemed like the hundredth time, the door rattled.

Horrified, Stella sprinted for the bend in the corridor and hurtled up the carpeted passage to the safety of the gym.

She dived inside, closed the glass door, and waited, breathlessly, until she heard the ping of the elevator arriving. Then she hustled back down the carpeted corridor and peered around the corner.

She was in luck.

Her heart raced even faster as she saw Juliet get into the elevator.

Was she alone? Stella thought she looked to be on her own.

Well, she hadn't been alone in that hotel room, that was for sure. So if she'd departed by herself, somebody else must still be there.

Stella wasn't at all sure that she was supposed to do this. In fact, she thought Roth might instruct her to do the opposite. But this was her only chance.

It could be dangerous. Nervously, she wished she had a weapon on her, thinking longingly of her trusty Glock, stashed away in its locker back at the academy. She hadn't thought she would need to have it with her when she was summoned to the director's office.

She would just have to do her best without it. Gathering her courage, she walked back to room two and tapped on the door.

CHAPTER SEVENTEEN

Stella's heart accelerated as she heard a throat clearing from inside the hotel room.

"You forgot something?" a voice asked.

The door opened and she stared into the astonished eyes of a young, dark-haired, good-looking man. He had his jeans on, though the belt was unbuckled, and his shirt was behind him, lying on the carpeted floor.

"Ma'am, I'm sorry, I thought you were…" His voice tailed off. "Who are you?" he asked, a new note of defensiveness in his voice.

Too late, Stella remembered that she had zero credentials. She didn't have a proper FBI badge. All she had was the ID card that all trainee agents had to wear at the academy. Usually, she kept it on a lanyard around her neck, but for now she'd stashed it away in a jacket pocket.

Stella decided not to use the card at all. She thought this man was young enough, and looked guilty enough, for her not to need it.

"I'm FBI Agent Fall, assisting with a murder investigation," she said, the official title sounding strange to her. "A woman, Amanda Logan, was stabbed yesterday morning in her home. Juliet Brand was a good friend of hers. We're checking out all friends and acquaintances and I saw her walk into this hotel. Now she walked out of the room, so she's been with you. What's your name, please?"

Stella made sure to adopt a businesslike tone. She wanted to come across as forcefully as possible so that he didn't try to wriggle out of the questioning, or refuse to answer.

But he seemed too thrown by her unexpected appearance to think of doing that.

"Tony," he stammered out. "Tony Cross."

He ran his fingers through his hair, looking distracted and worried. He really was very good-looking, Stella noted, and also younger than Juliet. She guessed he was in his early twenties.

"Tony, tell me, why did you meet with Juliet here?"

Of course, the discarded shirt and the crumpled bedcovers told an explicit story but she hoped that Tony might provide her with more of the whys.

"Isn't it obvious?" he shot back, sounding embarrassed.

"Why her? Why you? Why did this happen? How did you know her?" Stella probed.

He shook his head. "I'm as confused about it as you are, to be honest."

Looking shamefaced, he did up his belt, turned around, and reached for his golf shirt which he quickly pulled on.

"How can you be confused about it? Explain to me," Stella pushed.

He sighed, gazing down at the carpet as if he was regretting the impulsive decisions that had led him to this moment. "Look—look, I could really get into trouble for this, okay? Will it stay confidential?"

Stella tilted her head. "I guess that depends on what the information is, and whether it has any connection with the recent murder. If it doesn't, then yes, it will stay confidential."

"Well, I work for an electrical firm, Murray Arthur Electrics. I was hired earlier this year, just after I qualified. We did some work at the Brands' house recently. They needed the lighting in the living room changed. I was there two days last week. The first day with my boss and the second day on my own, finishing up. On the second day…" He paused, letting out a breath. "On the second day she really came onto me. Said I was cute. I mean, she really came on strong. She told me she'd call me if I was interested and we could get together."

"When did she call you?"

"Yesterday. She said I should give her a time and she'd tell me the place. So I did."

Now Tony's handsome features were glowing crimson.

"Just like that?" Stella asked.

Tony nodded. "This is seriously one of the weirdest experiences of my life. I mean, I got here, she arrived five minutes later. She—we, er—anyway, half an hour later she's dressed and walking out like none of this ever happened. I don't know what to make of it."

"She didn't say she wants to see you again?"

"No." Tony's short reply and outspread hands showed Stella clearly that he wasn't used to this. That he was pleased, yet hurt.

"Did any money change hands between you two?" Stella asked, wanting to rule this possibility out. Tony flushed even redder as if appalled by the question.

"Neither of us paid the other," he stated firmly.

"You didn't know her before this?"

"Honestly, I never saw her in my life. And it's the first time we've done work for her so please, please don't tell my boss. I'd get fired if he knew I'd done this. It's a big no to flirt with clients, especially married ones. He'd think I came onto her. Nobody would ever believe me if I told the truth."

Stella nodded. "I don't think it will be necessary to tell him. Thanks for your time."

As she left, she saw him turn away, rooting through the bedcovers, clearly looking for an item of clothing he'd mislaid during the action-filled half-hour.

She closed the door and headed downstairs, feeling as confused as the handsome Tony was.

What had played out in that hotel room felt so bizarre as to be surreal. It didn't make sense. And it definitely wasn't characteristic of the quiet, reserved, and rather introverted Juliet.

When Stella left the hotel, the first thing she saw was an annoyed-looking Roth, pacing up and down on the sidewalk on the opposite side of the road and glancing around expectantly.

With a pang, Stella remembered she'd defied his direct instructions. Roth had expected to find her out here, waiting for him. Quickly, she hurried over.

"Fall. Where have you been? What's happened?" he asked.

"I'm sorry. I decided to wait inside the hotel to see if I could find Juliet, and I did."

Roth sighed. "I didn't hear you ask me if you could do that. And you most definitely didn't hear my answer because I didn't give one."

"No, you're right. Next time I'll make sure to ask," Stella said, but she couldn't help thinking that her decision to ask for forgiveness rather than permission had at least gotten results.

But Roth was now seriously angry.

"In a situation like this, the team needs to know where each other is," he berated her. "This is a low-risk scenario, inasmuch as any scenario involving a murder investigation can be. But if you're being undisciplined and going off on a tangent in this instance, why should we trust you in a more dangerous one, where a shooter's on the loose, or it's a hostage situation?"

Stella felt deflated. Roth was right. She should have checked directly with him. She had been undisciplined, and thinking of her lack of discipline made her remember what was waiting for her back at the academy. An unpleasant mixture of fear and dread chilled her stomach again.

Roth then mitigated his criticism in a more level tone. "You may well have the better idea in a situation like this. You are on site, after all. But when it's a team effort, at least tell us. Then we know where you are and we can amend our plans accordingly instead of wasting time and worrying."

"I understand," Stella said contritely. "I promise I won't do it again."

"So. Now we have that cleared up, tell me what you saw upstairs," he said. "In fact, let's sit down."

He walked over to one of the restaurant's tables and motioned for Stella to take the opposite chair. "Bottle of water, please," he told the waitress.

"I knocked on the hotel room door after Juliet had left," Stella said.

She had a feeling Roth was holding back on his temper again. "My earlier warnings to you apply again. You're not authorized to do that yet. And you could have gotten yourself into danger."

"I know, and I won't do it again without asking first. But I did get results. I found the man she was with."

Stella took a sip of her water.

"And?" Roth's voice was challenging, as if he wanted to know exactly how this was helping the case.

"They'd met a few days ago. He was an employee at an electrical firm that they hired. She flirted with him while he was at the house, and then called him for a meet-up. He was very confused by it all. She was gone in half an hour."

Roth rubbed his chin thoughtfully.

"That doesn't sound like Juliet."

"I agree. And it doesn't sound like the first time she's done this."

Stella stared at him hopefully, relieved when he gave a reluctant nod.

"So she's a serial cheater. It might have a bearing on the case but I'm not sure how."

Stella drained her glass. Then she said, in pleading tones, "We really need to go talk to her, Roth."

He sighed. "It's not so simple. If we do, we show our hand, and we will more than likely learn nothing."

Stella shook her head. "I've been observing all three of the women during their questioning. Juliet is absolutely the one who'll be most vulnerable to pressure."

"Why do you say that?" Roth challenged her.

"She's the most unsure of the three. She doesn't trust herself as much as the others do and she's more easily influenced. She won't handle the pressure if we confront her with the evidence and she won't have the confidence, or bravado, to continue lying. She'll crack and she'll talk to us. And once she's talking, we might get other information we need."

Roth considered her words for a moment. Then he gave a decisive nod.

"Okay. Let's give it a go. Let's go and question her and tell her we know about her lunch hour hobby. And you'd better be right about her breaking. We need this woman to talk."

CHAPTER EIGHTEEN

Ten minutes later, Stella tapped on Juliet's door, feeling very nervous. The pressure was on. Roth expected her to get results. And Stella couldn't help remembering that she'd been wrong about one important aspect of Juliet's personality. She'd never pegged her as a cheater, which she was.

Had she even gone home afterwards? Stella felt sure she would have gone home, to shower and remove any physical evidence. But what if she hadn't, and they were unable to find where she was?

Tension coiled in her stomach as she wondered if she'd misread other crucial signals from this quiet and introverted woman. The confidence she'd felt ten minutes ago had now abandoned her.

Quick footsteps trod across the tiles, and a moment later Juliet opened the door.

She was wearing a pretty, white and gold top, and white tracksuit pants paired with flat sandals. She'd washed off a lot of the make-up Stella had seen earlier. She looked briefly startled to see the two of them.

"I'm so sorry, I didn't know you were coming back," she said.

"We have a couple of facts to check quickly." Stella smiled. "We were passing by. Sorry for the inconvenience."

"It's not a problem at all." Juliet rallied fast, but looked thrown by their arrival. She didn't want them to come in. She was still standing in front of the door, her body language betraying her words.

"May we come inside?" Stella asked politely.

As Juliet finally moved away to let them through, Stella noticed she had left her patterned jacket draped over a seat in the living room. There was something stuffed into one of the pockets, spoiling its elegant lines.

Juliet grasped the jacket and dithered momentarily before carrying it through to the hall. Then she returned to the living room.

"How can I help you?" she asked, smiling brightly. She was definitely out of her comfort zone, Stella realized. Looking at her demeanor, she felt more confident again. If she played her cards right, she hoped she could get to the truth.

“We actually came by earlier, just after lunch. It seems you weren’t in?” she asked.

Juliet flushed. Her cheeks glowed rosy pink.

“Yes, I had to run a few errands. I’m sorry. If I’d known you were coming back, I would have been here.”

“Where did your errands take you?” Stella asked.

She thought it was interesting that this time, Juliet hadn’t offered for them to sit, nor asked if they wanted refreshments. Subconsciously, she was feeling very uncomfortable and wanted them gone, pronto.

“I—how is that important?” Juliet asked. Stella could see she was thinking furiously, worried about lying, and now starting to fear that one of them might have seen her somewhere.

“Just asking. Getting an idea of your daily routine.”

“Well, my routine varies a lot. I don’t really do the same thing day to day.” She sounded defensive and miserable.

“Did you play rubber bridge, or sterling bridge, during your games?” Stella said, changing things up. As she’d expected, Juliet wasn’t the type to lie smoothly. She bit her lip and didn’t answer. The silence felt incredibly tense.

“Did you pass by the Kingsway Hotel at all while you were out today?” Stella asked.

Juliet gawped at Stella. Her indrawn breath was loud in the silence. Her flush was even more noticeable now. Her cheeks were deep crimson.

“What—what do you mean?” she said in a shaky voice.

“I can see you don’t want to lie. You’re trying very hard not to, ever since we’ve come back. Nothing so far that you have told us this afternoon has been a lie. But I’d like to know how much of the truth you’re going to tell us.”

“Please—” Juliet began, but Stella continued.

“Assume that we know everything. Otherwise, we may have to prompt you by telling you floors, room numbers, and various other details.”

Juliet blinked rapidly. Then her expression of rigorous control collapsed and she buried her face in her hands. Which, Stella noted, were shaking violently now.

“This can’t be happening. I don’t believe this is happening.”

She stumbled to the nearest chair and sat heavily down.

"That has nothing to do with the murder. It was just—just a crazy moment. It won't happen again. Please, I can't let Walter know. I can't. It will ruin our entire life. It will destroy everything. Everything."

She sounded aghast as she took in the consequences. Until that moment she'd been staring at the floor. Now, she raised her gaze to Stella and Roth in desperate appeal.

"You say it won't happen again. That's implying it's happened before?" Stella picked up. She couldn't tell from Juliet's reaction whether her guess was correct or not, as panic had made her shut down completely.

Deciding it was time for a sympathetic approach, and for some negotiation to start, Stella continued in a softer voice.

"It will be best if you tell us everything. If you are one hundred percent honest with us now, then we will keep this as confidential as we can. Unless it becomes necessary for the investigation, we won't tell your husband."

Juliet's face was now ashen. She stared at Stella through tear-filled eyes. Wanting for her to feel more secure at this critical moment, Stella perched herself on a seat to her right. Roth also recognized the need to diffuse the situation. He walked a few paces away and sat on a couch, further to the right. Stella thought that was a good choice. Now, Juliet wouldn't feel intimidated by their presence and could hopefully ease out of her crippling fear and open up. With any luck, they would now learn the truth about what had been going on.

"You promise?" Juliet asked one more time, sounding broken.

"You have my word," Stella confirmed.

Juliet let out a wobbly sigh. She stared at the floor for a long time, twisting her fingers together. Stella decided to be patient, and let her gather her thoughts. She sat as quiet and still as she could and finally, in a small, hoarse voice, Juliet began to talk.

"It started with Cassidy," Juliet said. "She was the first."

She stared at Stella in appeal. Stella nodded encouragingly.

"She was sick of her husband working such long hours, and suspected he was having an affair, so she cheated on him. She slept with someone who came around to fix her laptop. A cute young IT guy. She couldn't keep it a secret for long. She invited Eleanor and me for wine and she told us all about it."

"How long ago was this?"

"A few months ago."

"So this was before Amanda moved here?" Stella confirmed.

"Yes. It was just the three of us—Cassidy, Eleanor, and myself. We'd known each other for a couple of years, and were good friends."

"How did you and Eleanor respond?"

"I was shocked, and couldn't believe she'd done it. But Eleanor was in awe of her. I think secretly she was also feeling frustrated, as if her life was going nowhere. That's what she said. She laughed about it. She said she felt like her husband was more married to his work than her. And that's where it started."

"It did?" Stella asked.

"With three little words. 'I dare you,'" Juliet said in a trembling voice.

"So Cassidy dared Eleanor?" Stella confirmed.

"That's right," Juliet said sadly. "And at our next meet-up, Eleanor said she'd done it. She called up an old work colleague, from the days when she still had a job. They went for lunch and then they checked into a motel opposite. She said it was extraordinary. That it was the biggest adrenaline rush she'd had since she could remember. That she felt alive again."

Wow, Stella thought. She could see how this had escalated.

She didn't dare look at Roth. She didn't want to break the fragile connection with Juliet, which was now allowing the words to pour out.

"Then what happened?"

"Then I got the challenge. Eleanor told me, 'I dare you.'"

"And what did you do?"

"I refused the dare. I was quite upset by it, and it actually caused a few issues between us. We almost had a fight. But then my husband was out of town for a week. It was the third week in a month that he wasn't home. And I started realizing how lonely I was and how—how dull my life was. How pointless. Their words stuck in my mind. So I did it. There was a new personal trainer at the gym. He was only there for two weeks before leaving to train a sports team in another state. I had a session with him and he was flirty and very hot. I thought it wouldn't be difficult. So I decided to." Juliet sighed, fidgeting with the hem of her pretty top. "Afterward, I called the other girls and invited them for lunch. We have never laughed so much! It was like we were all friends again."

"And so after that, the dares continued?"

Looking shamefaced, Juliet nodded.

"We took turns. We'd get together afterwards and discuss all the details, I mean, everything! It's embarrassing to think what we said." She glanced doubtfully at Roth.

Stella couldn't help feeling appalled. Not only were the meet-ups themselves fraught with possible risk, but they also meant the potential destruction of these women's easy, comfortable lives. She was sure that Juliet, in particular, had started out being a victim of peer pressure after the other two had gotten involved. She could have said no, but that would have meant losing her friends.

"Did it escalate in any way?" she asked gently, hoping Juliet couldn't sense how shocked she was.

"Yes, it did," Juliet said, confirming Stella's suspicions that this would have happened. "I think it was Eleanor who decided we should start taking trophies, that it wasn't a proper dare unless we brought something home with us. Something personal belonging to the guy."

Stella thought of Juliet's jacket in the hallway and that odd bulge in the pocket.

"I took his bandana," Juliet said, as if reading her mind. "He wore a red bandana. I slipped it into my pocket before I left."

There was a short silence. Stella let it ride. Juliet had given them a wealth of information and she sensed she needed a minute to regroup.

"When did Amanda come into the picture?" she asked, when she felt Juliet was ready to continue.

"Cassidy met her first. She was new to the neighborhood and really sweet. She seemed quite innocent and of course, she was very pretty too. Cassidy thought she might like to join in, and I guess it was a bit of a head rush for all of us, because bringing in someone new was so risky."

They were becoming addicted to the risk, Stella realized. In their safe, mundane, privileged and yet inherently dull worlds, this truly had become the spark of excitement that had made them feel alive.

"Of course," Stella sympathized. "How did you do it?"

Juliet gave a short laugh, then looked surprised at herself, as if she hadn't thought such a thing was possible.

"We didn't at first. We were all too nervous. We invited her to join our group and for a few times, it really was just wine and gossip. But after a while, Cassidy started feeling her out. I mean, she introduced the subject in a very innocent way. Talked about how lonely we sometimes feel and asked her if she fantasized ever. She seemed okay with it. I mean, I thought she would probably go for it if she was challenged directly. And so, about a week ago, Cassidy did it. She spilled the beans about the latest affair she'd had and she said, 'I dare you.'"

Stella felt as if she hadn't moved a muscle for minutes. She was fascinated and appalled by how this had escalated.

The timing was so recent that it had to be significant, she thought, with cold certainty. Had those words somehow sealed Amanda's fate?

It was time for them to learn the critical information that this entire interview had built up to. That would be how Amanda had responded, and what had happened next.

But, at that moment, the front door rattled and then swung open. Footsteps tramped inside.

Immediately, Stella sensed Juliet tense. Terror emanated from her as she shut her mouth, swinging around on her seat.

"Hi, hon!" a man's voice called out. "Are you busy with someone?"

"It's Walter," Juliet whispered. "He's home."

CHAPTER NINETEEN

Stella had never been more frustrated by an interruption in her life.

She watched as Juliet's entire body tensed. Raw terror was emanating from her. They were on the point of a major breakthrough, but she'd made a promise. Juliet had trusted her enough to spill the story. Now, she couldn't break that trust.

She stood up and turned to greet the office-pale man staring curiously through the doorway at them. His expensive woolen suit jacket almost concealed his paunch.

"Afternoon, Mr. Brand."

"Good afternoon," he replied in a voice that held a hint of challenge, as if he wasn't pleased to arrive home and find strangers on his territory. His attitude sealed the decision for Stella.

"I'm Stella Fall and this is Special Agent Roth from the FBI. We've been asking Juliet some follow-up questions, looking for details she may have recalled about Amanda Logan's friends and contacts. We're all wrapped up now, so we can leave you to your family time."

She gave him a professional smile, aware of Roth drawing in a sharp, outraged breath behind her.

"Thank you for your help. We sure hope this gets resolved soon," he agreed, standing aside for them to leave.

Walter Brand was probably ten years older than Juliet. He looked like a serious type, Stella thought, taking in his demeanor and his conservative dress. But at the same time, he seemed a decent person who was innocent of his wife's misdoings. She felt sorry for both of them. Why couldn't life be more perfect? she wondered bitterly. Why did people have to do these things to mess it up?

She walked out, aware of Roth stomping out of the house behind her.

As soon as they'd climbed into the car, he let rip.

"Fall, what on earth was that all about? We were on the verge of a massive breakthrough."

Stella shrugged. "I know. But I made her a promise. I couldn't break it. It would be a breach of trust."

"Just one more question could have done it," Roth pressured. "I could easily have taken her husband aside."

"No. He didn't want us there. I sensed it immediately. He wouldn't have been happy to have been taken aside, and it would have put Juliet in a difficult situation. She wasn't in the right headspace to lie to him. Besides, we have two more witnesses to re-interview now," Stella reminded him. "It will actually be better to move on to someone else's version, as we can make sure the stories tally up. There's nothing stopping us coming back to Juliet later."

Roth sighed impatiently. "Point made. Okay, let's go, before Juliet gets some time alone with her cell phone and warns Eleanor and Cassidy about what's happening."

Stella agreed. There wasn't a moment to lose.

"Who's closest?" she asked, having a memory lapse about the locations of all the houses. All the driving around this unfamiliar suburb had disoriented her.

"Eleanor is closest."

"Shall we go there now?"

Stella reversed, and Roth checked the address, directing her on the short, zigzag route through suburbia. It was now early afternoon, and there was more activity on the streets. People were running, cycling, walking dogs. Groups of kids were heading down the sidewalks.

As they drove, Roth's phone beeped.

"Maxwell is in the area. Shall I tell him to meet us there?"

"Okay," Stella said. She felt in two minds about having Maxwell on the scene. She had renewed respect for Roth's experience, and his intuitive ability to handle the interview in a seamless way. Even when he'd disagreed with Stella, he'd waited until they were in the car to lay into her.

Realizing what it must have taken for this experienced agent to stay quiet and let a novice handle the interview, Stella felt grateful for the leeway he'd given her. She hoped she could do the same one day for somebody else. Even though she was sure Roth didn't like her and would take her off the case in a heartbeat, Stella acknowledged that this prickly man was a valuable role model.

She'd be lucky if she ever reached his level of wisdom and experience. That thought was humbling.

Maxwell, on the other hand, she was less sure about. He was fierier and less seasoned. Plus, their brief truce over burgers hadn't been enough to dispel his mistrust of her.

If Maxwell didn't control himself then the fragile trust she hoped to build with Eleanor would be shattered.

Although Stella reminded herself that Eleanor was a different person and the dynamic was likely to be completely different, too. She shouldn't assume what was likely to happen. They'd had many warnings about assuming during their training.

"Here we are." Roth interrupted her thoughts. He glanced in the rearview mirror as a car pulled up behind them. "And here's Maxwell."

They climbed out and Stella walked up to the front door, feeling under even more pressure now that Maxwell was here as well. Would anything go wrong? And most importantly, had Juliet managed to warn Eleanor what was happening?

She knocked, and a few moments later, Eleanor opened the door.

The puzzlement in her eyes told Stella that she genuinely didn't know why they were here and hadn't been forewarned by Juliet. Hopefully that was because Juliet's husband had been home, and she hadn't had a chance to sneak away and make the call.

"Afternoon." Stella smiled.

"You're back? What can I do for you? Is there something else you have to ask?" Her curious gaze encompassed all three of them before she stepped hurriedly aside.

"Come in, come in."

As Stella walked into the living room, she felt her heart thud into her shoes again. She'd assumed—wrongly, as it happened—that Eleanor would be alone, but she wasn't. A stocky man with salt-and-pepper hair was sitting on the couch, his laptop on the coffee table. He looked up inquiringly when he saw them.

"This is my husband, who's working from home for the next few days, until this crime is solved and we know we're safe. Steve, these are the FBI agents I was telling you about," Eleanor said, as Steve struggled hastily out of the couch's soft embrace to shake their hands.

"Afternoon, afternoon." Following the perfunctory handshake, Steve sat back down again and immersed himself in his work.

Stella stared at him in concern. He wasn't planning to leave while they spoke to Eleanor. This was unexpected and presented a massive obstacle.

"Do you want to sit?" Eleanor asked.

"Shall we go outside?" Stella remembered the deck where they'd been interviewed the last time. But Eleanor laughed dismissively.

"There's a wind today, so it's not going to be comfortable out there. One of our projects this fall is having it glassed in. For now, the living room is warmer."

Seeing the predicament, Roth stepped in.

"We don't want to interrupt your husband in his work. Is there somewhere else we can go?"

Given the size of the house, Stella was sure there were alternatives, but she also thought that Eleanor was resentful of them coming back again. On principle, and for no good reason, she was being obstructive.

"The living room is fine. Please, sit. Don't worry about Steve. He'll tune everything out if he's focused on work, won't you, honey?"

Steve barely nodded as he peered at rows of figures on the screen. Stella knew he might be focusing on work now, but he wouldn't for long. Not when the real reason for their visit became apparent.

"We prefer to question you in private, as there are certain facts in the case that are confidential," Stella said.

Eleanor put her hands on her hourglass hips and tossed back her short blond hair.

"Look here, you're the ones who pushed in again and interrupted our day. So you can fit in with us. Take a seat, ask your questions, and go. I'm not rearranging the entire house to accommodate you. Anything you say to me, you can say in front of Steve. It's not like I have anything to hide, and he's an actuary who knows about keeping things confidential."

She stared challengingly at Stella. Steve glanced up, nodded briefly in his wife's support, and then returned to his work.

Smiling, Eleanor sat on the opposite side of the couch and stared expectantly at the agents.

For one perplexing moment, Stella wondered if Steve did, in fact, know. Was theirs an open marriage? Were she and the agents going to lose the only advantage they had in terms of bargaining power; the leverage over the wife?

No, she told herself. It couldn't be like that. Not when the three friends had taken such glee in keeping their affairs a secret. Eleanor was simply blissful in her ignorance. She had no idea that they knew. That meant Stella would need to hint at where this was going, in order to give her one last chance to take it private.

"All right. This is the issue we need to discuss. I'll give you the background on it, Eleanor. Earlier today, one of your bridge friends left home and she headed to a hotel downtown. I was wondering if you might have any information on the trip? Were you told about this appointment?"

Now Eleanor had realized that the game was up. Stella saw panic fill her eyes. Her body language changed completely. She'd been lounging back on the cushions in a satisfied pose. Now she jumped up from her seat, tension furrowing her brow, her hands bunched in front of her.

"What friend? What are you insinuating?"

"Perhaps we could continue the conversation elsewhere?" Stella tried again, but it was no use. From her casual smugness, Eleanor had tipped all the way over into a blind panic from which there was no returning.

"Get out! I'm not answering any more of your questions."

"It's just background," Stella tried in a calm voice, but Eleanor could not be calmed.

"This is stupid and irrelevant. Who put you up to this? Some nosy, jealous neighbor wanting to cause trouble? You're not trying to solve the crime, you're trying to slander my friends. Is that what the FBI does these days? Tries to smear people's reputation by insinuating totally false facts?"

She stood face to face with Stella, her voice a shout. In her eyes, Stella could see the full extent of her terror. The knowledge about what she would lose. How close she was to having everything she was used to in her easy, pampered life come crashing down around her.

She sounded desperate, and in that moment, Stella knew that this woman was about to act impulsively. Perhaps she'd spill out some critical information, Stella thought, as Eleanor drew in a sharp breath.

CHAPTER TWENTY

"Screw you, bitch!" Eleanor shouted at Stella.

The next moment, her hand lashed out and she slapped Stella hard across the face.

Stella reeled back in shock, staggering away. She'd expected information, or some sort of a confession, not a vicious physical blow. Tears streamed from her eyes. Her cheek was burning.

"Ma'am, you just assaulted an FBI employee engaged in her official duties. We're arresting you," she heard Roth bark out.

There was a major commotion. Eleanor was screaming and struggling in the grip of Maxwell, who'd lunged forward to grab her arm. Blinking the tears away, still reeling from the assault, Stella tried to follow what was happening.

"Calm down, ma'am. Do not resist arrest or you'll make things even worse for yourself," Roth ordered, grasping Eleanor's other arm.

Maxwell had produced a pair of handcuffs from somewhere and the agents forced her hands in front of her and clipped them over her wrists.

"What the hell! What's happening?" her husband bellowed, jumping up from the couch. "You can't take my wife to jail!"

"Sir, we can and are. Assault is a federal offense that carries prison time." He turned to Stella. "Are you okay?"

A slap across the face could cause lasting eye damage. Stella knew, because the one time her mother had slapped her, she'd had blurred vision for days and had worried that her eye might never heal. Luckily Eleanor's blow had landed more across her cheek. It stung viciously, but her tears were from the sudden pain, nothing more.

"I'll be fine," she said.

"Get her in the car," Roth said, his tone conveying a complete lack of sympathy for the fact that Eleanor was now in screaming hysterics, staggering out of the house in Maxwell's grip as if her own legs could barely support her.

Steve pounded behind them, calling anxiously to his wife.

"Honey, this is outrageous. I'm contacting our lawyer immediately. Officers, are you taking her to the local precinct? We'll meet you there!"

Steve was standing outside the house, talking urgently on his phone, as they sped away, heading for the precinct.

Eleanor's screams abated as they drove. She lapsed into a silence punctuated by the occasional sob. Stella wondered whether she was crying from rage, or whether she'd finally begun to regret her actions. Either way, she hoped that when Eleanor was actually at the police station and taken into an interview room, reality would hit her hard enough to make her start talking.

*

Stella hesitated outside the interview room door, and Roth gave her a "you go first" gesture with his hand.

"I'll watch from the observation room," Maxwell whispered. "She might feel overwhelmed by the three of us. We need her to talk, and fast."

"Good call," Roth whispered back. "We might not have much time before the lawyer arrives, so let's see what we can get."

Nervously, Stella pushed open the door. It was quiet inside, but she fully expected a torrent of abuse the moment Eleanor set eyes on her.

To her surprise, the blond woman was huddled in her chair, looking deflated and scared.

"I'm sorry. I'm so sorry, honey," she said in a small voice.

As Stella approached, remorseful tears began streaming from her reddened eyes.

Roth walked around the table and removed her handcuffs. Then he passed her a box of Kleenex before glaring sternly at her.

Eleanor shrank away from him, turning back to Stella.

"I had to do something. I had no idea you knew about—about everything. I panicked. All I could think of was that I had to stop you saying another word. Please don't press charges against me. Is your face okay? I can see it looks red."

Crumpling the tissue, she stared anxiously from Stella to Roth and back again.

With her handcuffs now removed, Eleanor's manicured fingers were laced tightly in front of her. Stella noticed that in the struggle with the agents, she'd broken a nail.

Now, with Eleanor firmly on the back foot, Stella had a big advantage. Furthermore, Eleanor had no idea which of her friends had confessed. For all she knew, both had. This, too, could provide valuable leverage.

"We know what happened in your get-togethers. We know about the dares, and the trophies," Stella said sternly.

Eleanor winced as if Stella had raked her nails across her face. She flushed, looking deeply uncomfortable.

"We know you introduced Amanda to the group and that you ladies waited a while before giving her a challenge." She narrowed her eyes at Eleanor.

Her response was a forlorn nod. "Yes. That's what happened."

"Tell us truthfully. What was Amanda's reaction when Cassidy dared her? Describe it in your words." Stella made sure to emphasize the "your" to reinforce Eleanor's belief that both her friends had already described it in their words.

Eleanor sighed.

"Let me just—let me get my head straight. I don't want to say anything factually wrong and land myself in even more trouble. Can I have some water?"

Stella got up and poured a glass from the jug on the shelf. She handed it to Eleanor, who gripped it tightly with both her shaking hands.

The large diamond in her ring flashed as she lifted the glass and drank.

"Okay. Amanda. That get-together. We were all so nervous about asking her to do it. But the thrill, the anticipation, was part of the fun. We were all knocking back the bubbly to give us courage. Juliet had organized a couple of bottles of Moet and I don't think any of us bothered with the orange juice. Anyway, Cassidy eventually spilled the beans and gave the dare and I must say, Amanda responded very weirdly. It wasn't the way I expected her to react at all."

Stella knew that she mustn't give away that she had no idea as yet how Amanda had reacted.

"Tell me your version of events," she said, again emphasizing the "your." "I want your personal impressions of how it played out."

Eleanor didn't seem in the least suspicious that she was telling them brand new information as she replied.

"Well, as I recall, first Amanda laughed. But she did it in a disbelieving way. As if she was sure it was a joke but not entirely sure.

Then, when we didn't laugh with her, she realized it was serious and that we meant it."

"What did she do then?"

"She asked us to tell her more. To explain exactly what we'd all been doing. So we did," Eleanor said in a small voice. "We were pretty drunk by then and she seemed to be laughing with us by that stage, so we told her everything we'd done. We spilled it all to her. The dares. The meet-ups."

"And then?" Roth asked. His voice was interested and warm, without any trace of the earlier hardness. Clearly he was focused on getting Eleanor to relax and open up. "How did Amanda respond to that?"

Eleanor stared at him, looking thoughtful. "Then I think she realized that she was trapped. She had to go along with it, and if she didn't then the friendship would be over. That was what I picked up, anyway. And Cassidy hinted at it, too. She said something about how Amanda needed to do it if she wanted to keep her group of friends."

"That's more of an ultimatum than a hint," Stella observed, thinking that Cassidy had a toxic side she'd kept carefully hidden during the interview with the FBI.

"I guess it was. An ultimatum," Eleanor agreed miserably.

Perhaps it had also been construed as a threat, Stella thought.

Roth nodded and scribbled something in his notebook.

She could imagine it must have been a shocking time for Amanda. She'd realized her friends weren't who she thought they were. She'd been threatened by Cassidy. Plus, she knew things would be very different for her if she didn't accept the challenge. A refusal would not have been well received.

She was sure now that Amanda hadn't accepted the challenge. Something had gone wrong between the friends. She could see it in Eleanor's body language, her slight frown, the way she glanced down at the floor as if she was ashamed.

"What happened next?" she asked.

"Amanda stood up. She stared at us all with this strange look on her face. I felt very small, as if she was calling me out for being a bad person. And then she said she refused to take part. She said she thought we were all two-faced cheaters. That there was no way she was going to do this."

"Then what?" Stella asked.

"That comment escalated things. Cassidy got defensive. She started trying to pressure her, saying it was just a little game, and that if she didn't go along with things she'd be ostracized, that we'd all close ranks against her, that she'd never make friends in this town and if she tried to tell anyone what had happened, nobody would believe her. But Amanda didn't listen. She looked absolutely furious. She turned and walked out."

Stella tried to imagine how the dynamic in the room had felt at that point. What had the group's reaction been when she left?

"What were you thinking at the time?" she asked.

"I felt terrified by how she reacted. I thought we'd messed up badly. For a moment I was scared that maybe she was planning to go and tell our husbands. But then I reassured myself that she didn't know any of them well. She'd never met my husband or Juliet's, and had only said hello to Cassidy's husband once or twice in passing at her place. So she'd just look like a jealous troublemaker. When she'd left, we all discussed it and tried to reassure ourselves of that."

"Did you go not after her, try to call her to come back?"

"None of us quite took in what had happened until she'd gone. Like I said, it was so different than we'd expected, and we were shocked. I think we were all feeling afraid, like we'd done something really stupid and now we couldn't take it back. Cassidy tried to call her but she didn't pick up. We didn't expect her to."

"And did you hear from her again?"

"No. Not so much as a phone call. We were supposed to have met up again today, in fact, it was one of our regular days. I didn't expect her to be there, none of us did, but a small part of me couldn't help hoping that perhaps she'd rethought, and she was going to arrive, and everything would be okay between us again. But there was something in the way she looked at us before she left that told me it wouldn't; that it was never going to be the same for any of us. Call it a premonition." Eleanor shivered. "Obviously we canceled as soon as we heard she was murdered."

Stella couldn't help suppressing a shiver, too. What had played out at that drunken "bridge" gathering was weird. It had veered off-course and taken a bizarre turn. Stella had assumed that she would have accepted the dare and it had somehow led to her murder. But the opposite had happened. What had Amanda been thinking when she left?

Perhaps that was the wrong question. Maybe a better question was what the other three friends had been thinking, and what they had decided to do after Amanda had left. Because that pointed to a strong motive for murder, Stella thought, with a flare of excitement.

CHAPTER TWENTY ONE

Roth cleared his throat, and glancing at him, Stella saw that he had reached the same logical conclusion.

"Where were you on the night Amanda was killed?" he asked Eleanor in harsh tones.

She gaped at him, looking shell-shocked.

"You're accusing me? I would never have done such a thing!"

But she could have, Stella realized. She was right-handed. That was why the left side of her face still felt on fire from the slap.

"I am not accusing you—yet. But I am asking you an important question. If you three told Amanda what you'd done, and she walked out after making it clear she was angry and disapproving, that represented a very real risk to you, your relationships, your way of life. All of you had a potential motive to make sure she never told on you."

"Like I said, we would have closed ranks. Her version against ours." Eleanor sounded panicked. "We'd have made up stories to discredit her. Cassidy can be cruel that way. None of us would have killed her!" Eleanor protested.

"Even so, do you have an alibi? Or were you home alone?"

"I do have an alibi," Eleanor said.

"What were you doing?"

"I was with Juliet," she said hurriedly.

"You were?" Roth pressured.

Stella felt a moment's disappointment that if the alibi held up, then both she and Juliet would be cleared.

"Our husbands were working late, so we decided to head out for dinner and a movie. We were both feeling upset about things. We wanted to forget about the whole debacle for a while. We asked Cassidy but she said she was busy." Eleanor stared at him appealingly.

She was fidgeting with her wedding ring, twisting the gold band around on her finger. Stella wondered whether it was a nervous habit, or whether she subconsciously wanted to hold onto this symbol of her marriage.

"So it was the two of you?"

"Yes. We took a cab to Norwalk. We watched the movie first and then we had an eight p.m. booking at Lorenzo's, which is an Italian restaurant that we both love. We know the owner well. He can confirm we were there. We got home at about eleven. We were both quite drunk."

"Thank you," Roth said.

At that moment, there was a minor commotion outside the interview room.

The door was flung open, and Stella watched in surprise as a determined-looking, gray-haired man in a tailored black suit appeared in the doorway. He was closely followed by Maxwell, who looked stressed.

"Sir, this is an FBI interview! You can't just barge in."

"I am here to represent my client, on the behest of her husband," the man thundered. His gaze lit on Eleanor. "Mrs. Lane, you have the right to remain silent. Don't say a word until I have dealt with these agents. I'm going to get you out of here and back home in the shortest possible time!"

Roth stood up.

"Good morning, sir. FBI Special Agent Roth. We brought your wife in as a precautionary measure. She has been very helpful in confirming a few facts. There is no reason for us to hold her here any longer and she is released. We are bringing no charges against her."

The lawyer looked taken aback, as if he'd worked himself up to win a fight that had just been canceled.

Eleanor then stood up.

"You're so kind to have gotten here so quick, Adam," she said soothingly. "Thank you for your help."

Without a backward glance at the FBI team, she headed out the door, closely followed by Adam. Their footsteps retreated down the passage.

Maxwell stepped inside the interview room and closed the door again. With a pained sigh that told Stella exactly what he thought of lawyers in general and Adam in particular, he sat down on the chair Eleanor had occupied.

"Well, that interview certainly gave us more insight," Roth said thoughtfully. "I'll ask Detective Grant to confirm with the restaurant that Juliet and Eleanor really went on that girls' night out. I guess the other option would be whether they hired someone."

Stella nodded, impressed by Roth's attention to detail and how he seemed to be aware of every possible loophole a suspect might try to use.

"However, I don't see Amanda opening the door to a stranger at night," Roth continued.

"A hit man would also have brought his own weapon. Not used one of the family's kitchen knives," Maxwell observed. "So we probably don't need to pursue that line of thinking any further with Juliet and Eleanor."

"But that leaves Cassidy," Stella said, exchanging a glance with Maxwell.

"Exactly," Maxwell agreed.

"Where was she that night?" Stella asked. "She was the ringleader who'd escalated the whole situation with her threats. Never mind what they said about how Amanda would have been a social pariah and would never have told on them. That's just what they hoped would happen. The truth was Amanda now possessed very damaging information and she not only refused the dare but also told them what she thought of their actions."

"According to what Eleanor said, Cassidy couldn't join them for dinner and a movie on the night of the murder because she was busy," Roth said.

"Busy doing what?" Stella said excitedly.

"I agree she has the biggest motive, since she threatened Amanda directly," Maxwell emphasized.

Stella felt surprised, but glad, to have him backing up her theory.

Roth nodded. "Okay. There are three of us, so that means we can look in separate directions. You two can track Cassidy down and speak to her. I'm going to look over the case notes again and try to find details we may have missed."

Stella felt pleased to have been tasked with tracking Cassidy down, even though she didn't know where Cassidy was, or how they would find her. She glanced at Maxwell as Roth left the room, hoping he didn't mind being partnered with her. She didn't think that was what he'd wanted at all, but she felt relieved to have someone else with her, especially the resourceful and fast-thinking Maxwell.

Maxwell clearly didn't mind. As soon as Roth was gone, he leaped into action.

"We need to locate Cassidy urgently. You say you lost her on her way through town?"

"Yes. For all I know she might be back home by now."

"Okay. Step one, let's call her landline and see."

Stella liked this practical approach.

Maxwell stood up. He and Stella hustled through to the back office. Having found Cassidy's number, Maxwell dialed her landline.

"Hello," he said, when someone answered. "Is Cassidy there?"

He waited. His lips tightened impatiently. Stella frowned. Was there a problem?

"Is your mommy there?" Maxwell asked again, fake bonhomie dripping from his words.

"No, I don't know where your mommy is. Do you know where your mommy is? Would you be able to call somebody who could tell me?" He paused, impatience radiating from him as he listened. "My favorite color? I don't have a favorite—okay, wait. It's blue. My favorite color is blue. Now, do you know where—oh, is your favorite color pink? That's great. Nice choice. Do you know where your mommy is?"

Then his features relaxed, and relief replaced the tension she was seeing.

"Hi, hi. Yes, no problem, the kid was very charming. I'm calling from the FBI team. We're looking for Cassidy. We want to confirm a detail from the interview earlier." He paused, listened. "Okay, when do you expect her? She didn't say? No problem. It's not urgent, we'll try again later."

He cut the call with a disappointed sigh.

"The au pair finally came on the line. She doesn't know where Cassidy is, but it doesn't sound unusual. Seems she comes and goes as she likes during the day."

"Do we have a cell phone number for her?" Stella asked.

Maxwell nodded decisively.

He picked up the phone and dialed. A moment later he shook his head.

"Voicemail. Must be turned off. So our next step is to head out and look for her."

"I can show you on a map where I lost her. She can't have gone far if she was heading into town. She must have been going to a restaurant or a gym, or maybe the hairdresser?"

"Good point. We can check out possible destinations," Maxwell agreed.

“We have to be careful how we approach her, because she’s the leader of the three and she’ll be the most accomplished liar,” Stella warned. “Plus, she’s had the most time to be warned. Either Eleanor or Juliet has probably gotten hold of her by now and told her what’s happened.”

Maxwell nodded thoughtfully.

“I was also wondering, I know it doesn’t seem very likely, but what if Amanda ended up taking the dare?” Stella asked.

“She didn’t sound like she was going to,” he countered.

“But nor did Juliet. That’s why I suddenly thought it would be worth looking into the possibility. Remember, Juliet also refused outright, but she didn’t take long to come around to the idea. Amanda could have left in a huff, and then regretted her temper outburst, and started thinking what it would mean to lose her new friends. They had second thoughts about what had happened. Maybe she did too.”

“What are you implying? She took the dare—so what?”

“She might have hidden a trophy somewhere,” Stella said. “Remember what a big fuss they made about the trophies? Amanda would have needed that proof.”

Maxwell bumped his fist against his chin thoughtfully.

“Yes. But it might be very hard to trace something like that back. How would you know if it’s a trophy or just a pair of Craig’s underpants?”

“I guess finding something hidden would be a starting point. Even if they’re unlikely to be monogrammed with the wearer’s full name and business address,” she joked.

Maxwell’s lips twitched.

“Okay then. If you want to take a look around for anything, I’ll work on Cassidy’s location. Show me where you lost her. I know the area slightly and can pinpoint any places where she might logically have gone. I’m guessing a hotel room meet-up wasn’t on the cards or she’d have been home already.”

Just as she thought she had a partner on the case, they were already going their separate ways. Stella felt surprisingly disappointed before common sense rushed in. Of course they had to chase different angles, seeing the day was already wearing on.

She showed Maxwell on the map exactly where Cassidy had made her impatient left-hand turn.

"Call me if you find where she is. And I'll call you if I discover any evidence that Amanda changed her mind and went ahead with the dare."

Stella headed to Detective Grant's desk and signed out the Logans' front door key, which the police had taken so that they could access the scene.

"Will Mr. Logan be there?" she asked him.

"No, no. He's staying in a hotel in town for a few days. He didn't want to go home so he booked himself into the Marriott. Just make sure you leave everything as you found it and lock up carefully," Grant warned.

Stella pocketed the envelope. Then she left the precinct and headed on the short route back to the Logans' home.

As she drove, her butterflies fluttered up again. It felt like an intrusion to be going into a house and searching through someone's personal belongings without knowing what she was looking for. And it was scary and creepy returning to a crime scene, Stella thought, as she turned onto Begonia Drive. The tape strung around the porch pillars was a brightly colored warning that tragedy and murder had occurred here.

Stella ducked under the tape, which was fluttering in the cool breeze, and unlocked the door.

She stepped inside, holding her breath.

This was going to be the equivalent of finding a needle in a haystack. So she would have to think the same way that Amanda might have thought.

Closing the front door behind her, Stella stood for a moment in the cool gloom.

Who was Amanda, really?

She still didn't have any sense of her as a person at all. Craig's shell-shocked account hadn't been descriptive, and all Amanda's friends had been collaborating in a lie. So a lot of what she did know, Stella realized, might be inaccurate. The most truthful moment had been Eleanor's description of how Amanda had responded to the dare.

Stella got the impression that Amanda had been secretive. She'd shown one face to the world—but the other face? What was that really like? A secretive person would have secrets to hide. Assuming that was the case, where would they be hidden?

Somewhere that her husband wouldn't look, Stella thought. But also, somewhere close by. Because that was the person she was.

Stella hesitated, glancing at the kitchen. Had Amanda been a domestic goddess who adored cooking? She hadn't had that impression and Craig hadn't mentioned it. So the kitchen wasn't her personal domain.

It would have been the bedroom. Somewhere in the bedroom.

Stella climbed the stairs, feeling reluctant about going back into the place where this had happened. Her arms were already prickling into goose bumps as she walked toward the bedroom door.

Stepping inside, she saw the stripped, squeaky clean base of the bed standing on sparkling floorboards. The mattress and bedding had been removed and a thorough clean had been done. It was less nerve-racking to work in this silent and sanitized space.

Stella's first guess was the bedside table. What side had Amanda slept? The bloodstains had been on the side nearest the door.

But when she checked the drawer under the table, it looked as if that had been Craig's side. Stella walked around the bed to Amanda's side, but it yielded only a pack of Kleenex and a pair of dangly gold earrings which she guessed Amanda had taken off last minute, rather than sleep with.

Then Stella's gaze was drawn to the white vanity table on the far side of the room, near the window. That would be another private and exclusively feminine place that would have been Amanda's own.

There were a few cosmetics and hairsprays set out on its clean and tidy top, a container of make-up brushes, a hairbrush, and a couple of perfume bottles. Stella guessed there'd be more in the narrow drawer.

She opened it. Yes, here was Amanda's messy side, invisible from view and concealed. Perhaps the cleaner kept the visible areas neat, because the drawer was a jumble of lipsticks and eyeshadows, half-finished powder compacts, hairpins, used Kleenex, eye pencil stubs, and even a few items of jewelry that must have been hastily stashed here instead of in their proper place.

Stella felt perplexed as she stared down at this mess. How was it possible? Amanda had just moved! Hadn't she organized her stuff before packing it away? Then she grimaced in wry amusement at her own confusion. In fact, she should be glad to see this disaster area of a drawer, because it proved to her very clearly that there were two different sides to Amanda. There was the side the world saw, and then a hidden one.

She was about to close the drawer when she noticed something, half-concealed by a lipstick-marked Kleenex.

It was a tiny black book, not much bigger than a Post-it note, and surely too small to be practical. Stella picked it up and with delicate fingers, opened it.

The first few pages were filled with writing in a distinctive, bright blue hand. There were dates and initials, she realized, but she had no idea what they meant. There was the pen she'd used, in the corner of the drawer, disguised among several eyebrow pencils and lip liners.

As Stella was trying to puzzle out what this could be for, her phone rang. The sound was so sudden, and her focus so intense, that she jumped and almost dropped the book.

It was Maxwell calling. Quickly, she answered.

"Are you in there?" He sounded excited, revved up.

"Are you outside?" Stella said, surprised.

"I'm on my way past, and I've just pulled into the driveway. Come outside, quick. I've found where Cassidy is."

"I'll be there now!" Stella told Maxwell hurriedly. She slipped the booklet into her pocket, not wanting to leave it behind, and closed the vanity's drawer.

Then she sprinted downstairs and ran out of the Logans' house.

"Follow me," Maxwell called, leaning out of his window. "She's at a day spa on the other side of town. I asked the staff to do whatever they could to keep her there. They said they would try."

Stella jumped into her unmarked and set off behind him.

CHAPTER TWENTY TWO

A few minutes later, Maxwell burned rubber pulling into a stately entrance, with Stella hot on his heels. The pillared gateway led to a central fountain, with paved parking to the left and right. The parking lot was still quite full. Cassidy drove a silver Volvo, Stella remembered. She could see a few Volvos among the other luxury vehicles.

Maxwell parked in the closest bay to the main entrance and Stella pulled up beside him. They climbed out and hurried in. Stella was hastily arranging her thoughts. They'd need to get Cassidy alone. Perhaps there'd be an available treatment room where they could sit. She wanted somewhere quiet, peaceful, and out of the public eye.

The reception desk was surrounded by greenery. A trickling fountain flowed down a feature wall beyond. The place felt hushed, peaceful, and top-end luxurious.

"Afternoon. FBI Special Agent Maxwell." Even Maxwell lowered his voice when entering this serene domain. Discreetly, he showed the receptionist his badge. "I called earlier. We're here to interview Mrs. Cassidy Cooper," he said in low tones.

"Yes, of course." The immaculately groomed receptionist flashed pearly teeth in a smile. "She's in the Oyster Bar. It's to the right."

She indicated a wide archway wreathed in greenery and highlighted by a constellation of mini spotlights.

"Thank you."

Maxwell marched into the bar.

Stella paused and asked the helpful receptionist, "Is there anywhere private we might be able to speak? Perhaps a treatment room that isn't currently occupied?"

"Of course!" The receptionist smiled again. Stella guessed she saw the wisdom in keeping FBI agents out of the public's eye. "Let me have a look for you. We have a couple of rooms that are free at this time."

She turned to her computer screen and began searching, but at that moment, Maxwell marched out of the Oyster Bar.

Stella was taken aback to see he was alone. He looked angry.

"Mrs. Cooper is not in the bar. Do you know where she is?"

"Not in the bar? But she told me she was going in. She just came past now. Not two minutes ago!" the receptionist protested. "Are you sure she's not there?" She peered anxiously through the archway as if her gaze might summon her up.

"Yes, I'm sure." Maxwell turned to Stella. "She must have left. I think someone told her we were coming."

He glared at the receptionist, who looked horrified.

"I assure you, sir, we didn't warn her of anything! Her treatments only finished a few minutes ago."

"Someone warned her," Maxwell argued. Stella agreed. Her money was on one of Cassidy's friends, rather than a spa employee. She must have looked at her phone after her treatments and realized the game was up. Even so, this was not the time to debate whose fault it was, but rather for more practical action.

"If she's only just left, we might be able to catch her. Maybe she's on the way to her car."

Maxwell nodded decisively.

"Silver Volvo, number plate ends in XR. You take the left, I'll take the right."

He sprinted out. Stella followed, hot on his heels.

She turned right, but as she started scanning the number plates, she heard Maxwell shout, "FBI! Stop!"

Stella spun around to see him in the parking lot, standing in the path of a silver Volvo that was departing at speed. Only Cassidy was clearly not stopping for anyone. Tires screamed. Stella saw her hands vividly through the windshield, white shapes locked onto the wheel. At the last moment, in sheer self-preservation, Maxwell leaped desperately to the right, landing in a crouch as lithely as a cat.

Horrified, Stella realized that Maxwell's quick reactions had narrowly saved him from injury. Cassidy's actions had been nothing short of murderous. How could you accelerate when someone stood in your path? Stella felt stunned by what she'd witnessed.

She rushed back to Maxwell's unmarked, thinking that they would have to chase her down, but at that moment another departing guest reversed out of a bay near the gate, ahead of the speeding Cassidy, blocking her way.

Cassidy blared her horn, rubber squealing as she braked, and Stella saw her chance.

Rushing up to Cassidy's car, she wrenched open the passenger door and dived inside. The seat was plush and cool. The interior smelled faintly of deliciously fragranced spa ingredients. And Cassidy's wrath felt like an actual force as she glared furiously at Stella.

"Get out!" she yelled.

"Mrs. Cooper, please stop the vehicle and speak to Agent Maxwell! You're disobeying a federal agent's instructions, and you're going to be in big trouble."

"I'm not stopping! How dare you climb in without permission? You're violating my rights and carjacking me. I said, get out!"

Cassidy shoved her violently, and almost succeeded in pushing her out, as Stella hadn't yet closed the door. She shrieked as she fell backward, making a desperate grab at the seat. She missed, and her heart leaped into her mouth as the car accelerated. She was literally going to be thrown from a moving vehicle.

But then her other flailing arm brushed against the door's inner handle and she grabbed at it, saving herself from the fall, managing to wriggle her legs back in. Cassidy was powering along, swerving left and right, clearly doing her best to dislodge Stella, but she had purchase now, and a moment later she managed to slam the door.

Now she was alone in the car with a woman driving like a demented speedster.

"Stop, please!" Stella begged. She didn't have her belt on and if they crashed, she would be on a one-way trip through the windshield. And the way Cassidy was driving, that seemed likely. She was either in panic mode, or in a killing rage.

"You can't threaten me! You have no right to order me to stop!"

She swerved down a side street and flattened her foot. She was going way too fast, insanely fast, this was reckless beyond belief. Stella made a grab for the wheel but Cassidy clawed at her hand, her long, crimson nails digging into her flesh. Tires wailed on the blacktop. For a stomach-twisting moment she felt the car start to slide. They were in the oncoming lane, she realized, panic turning to gut-wrenching fear. Horns blared and she saw the other cars swerve desperately out of their path.

Then the Volvo righted itself on the road, fishtailing as Cassidy mashed her foot on the pedal again. The road seemed to telescope in front of her as they flew ahead. They were approaching a stop sign and with a sense of doom, Stella knew they were not going to stop, or even slow. If there was oncoming cross-traffic, they would end up in a horror crash.

"Stop, stop, stop!" she screamed, hearing the terror in her own voice, but Cassidy seemed deaf to her words, and oblivious to the perils of her actions.

It was like watching a terrible accident play out, only she was part of it, Stella thought, shouting in helpless fear as they sped through the intersection, an outraged blast of the horn telling Stella that they'd missed a serious collision by a fraction of a second.

"You are going to kill us both!" Stella yelled. "Stop the car! Stop now!"

"Get away from me!" Now Cassidy was driving with one hand and fighting Stella off with the other. This was going to end in absolute disaster. There was no way they were going to escape this insane ride unharmed, and it was clear that in the moment, Cassidy didn't care what happened.

In a flash, she saw her chance and knew what action she had to take to try and save them. It was the only choice.

Lunging in front of Cassidy, grabbing her wrist in a death-grip, Stella snaked her foot into the driver's side and stamped it on the brake pedal as hard as she could.

It was like hitting a wall. Cassidy was flung forward as the tires screamed and smoked. Her head cracked against the steering wheel and she reeled sideways, briefly stunned. Stella used the moment to jam the car into Park and put the hazards on. She was breathing as hard as if she'd run a hundred-yard dash. They were stopped diagonally in the slow lane of a four-lane main road, obstructing traffic, but at least they were at a standstill. Until she got Cassidy out of the car, she wasn't going to dare to move. Stella kept her shaking hand clamped protectively over the gear stick as horns blared around her.

Spots floated in front of her eyes and she felt dizzy. She couldn't believe they had survived. That ride had been the scariest experience of her life. And now Cassidy was sitting up, rubbing her forehead, looking dazed and angry.

"What the hell did you try and do there?" she snapped at Stella. "You carjacked me! Get out, bitch! I'm going to call my lawyer."

She shook her blond hair back angrily.

There was a raw viciousness in her words that Stella hadn't sensed, or even imagined, she possessed. Cassidy's plentiful charm was simply a veneer. Underneath it, Stella was shocked by the real person that had been revealed.

Sirens blared behind her. She turned to see Maxwell speeding up. He'd activated the lights on his unmarked, too. He braked hard as he reached her, jumped out, and sprinted over.

Maxwell pulled the driver's door open and before Cassidy could realize what was happening, he grabbed her arms and swiftly and expertly clicked a pair of handcuffs over her wrists.

"You okay?" he asked Stella, and she could hear the tension sharpening his voice.

"I'm fine," she said, but she had to shout out the word, because Cassidy was screaming again, yelling insults and profanities at the top of her voice. The sound waves battered Stella's eardrums and spittle showered over her face.

This reaction was completely excessive, Stella thought. Either Cassidy was an entitled princess at a level far removed from reality—or she had something to hide.

This seemed like a guilt response. What was she guilty of? Was it just her affairs that she was trying to hide?

Or was she the killer?

CHAPTER TWENTY THREE

Stella climbed out of her unmarked at the police precinct, in time to watch a shouting and screaming Cassidy being unloaded from the van that had transported her there.

"When are you going to let me call my lawyer? You do realize everything you've done is completely illegal?"

Maxwell helped her out of the van. Detective Grant, who'd driven Cassidy's Volvo to the police station, was waiting to take the other arm of the still-struggling woman.

"Please come this way, ma'am," Detective Grant insisted, in polite but firm tones. "It will be easier for all of us, and go better for you, if you don't resist."

With an impatient sigh, Cassidy flipped her hair back, but she stopped fighting and trailed defiantly along between the two men.

The sergeant at the main desk buzzed the side door open. They led Cassidy into a small interview room, where Maxwell and Grant maneuvered Cassidy around the desk to the single chair on the opposite side, and sat her down.

Roth rushed into the interview room from the back office, looking excited.

"All yours, ladies and gents," Detective Grant said in a relieved voice as he hustled out, leaving Cassidy with the three of them.

"Why am I being arrested?" Cassidy asked in a piercing voice. Venom oozed from the words. "I should already have had the chance to call my lawyer. I know my rights! I know the law a lot better than it seems you do!"

"You're not being arrested—yet," Maxwell said, and there was a quietly threatening note to his voice. "We have ample grounds to do so. Reckless endangerment. And failing to obey a federal officer. These are serious offenses and they carry significant jail time. But for now we are detaining you. We will then decide whether to press charges."

Stella thought it was Maxwell's calmness, even more than his words, that quelled Cassidy's attitude. She closed her pretty mouth and Stella could see her thinking furiously, trying to figure a way out of her predicament.

“I suppose you already found out about our innocent little activities?” she asked eventually, but she seemed more subdued. She directed the question at Stella, who replied, trying to keep as calm as Maxwell.

“We already know about the dares, and the affairs. And the trophies,” she said in level tones. “We know that Amanda refused your dare and criticized you, despite you threatening her that your group would ostracize her if she did. That must have been a shock. I’m sure you realized the risk it meant to you, your marriage, your way of life and social standing.”

Cassidy was struggling to maintain that straight-faced poise.

“So you know all this already. In that case, you invaded my car and my life for what reason?” The words were defiant but her tone was unsure.

“I want to know where you were on the night Amanda Logan was murdered. That’s all,” Stella said.

Cassidy pressed her lips together. She frowned. Looking closely, Stella could see signs of new tension around her eyes and mouth. She wasn’t aggressive now. Rather, she was worried.

“Why do you need to know?” she said.

“Were you home?” Stella pressed. “Or, if we asked, would we find that your au pair looked after the kids that evening?”

“I told you. I’m not willing to disclose it. I have a right to privacy.”

“You didn’t join your friends for dinner and a movie. You told them you were busy. Busy doing what, exactly?”

“I can’t remember. You guys have just illegally detained me, and you now expect me to list all my activities every day this week?”

“The evening in question was only two nights ago. It shouldn’t be difficult to recall,” Maxwell emphasized.

Cassidy shrugged silently.

“Were you off on a dare? Sleeping with a stranger?” Maxwell queried. “If so, I understand you don’t want to say. But unfortunately, thanks to your earlier actions, it will now go into the official case records, and that means your husband will know. However, if you are willing to tell us now, there might be no reason to keep you here. We could release you without charges.”

Now Cassidy was blinking. Her bravado was ebbing. But still, she didn’t take the offer. Instead, she stared back in angry silence.

Stella was becoming more and more convinced she was the killer.

"Perhaps my guess is wrong and you weren't on a dare. Perhaps you were making sure that your dares never got found out," Stella suggested.

Her words cracked Cassidy's defensive veneer. Again, she exploded.

"Amanda got what she deserved. She's no better than us, and she fooled herself if she thought she was. You know what they say. Snitches get stitches." She tossed her hair back again and raised her handcuffed hands to tease a stray strand away from her temple.

It was sticking there because she'd started to sweat.

"Did you give her those stitches?" Stella asked.

"I refuse to answer until my lawyer arrives. I know my rights, woman," Cassidy sneered.

Incredibly, even backed up against the ropes, Cassidy was taking the chance to be condescending and superior.

"Did you speak to Amanda after that bridge session where you dared her?" Roth asked.

"I did not." Cassidy raised her chin, looking down her nose at Roth.

Then Roth continued, innocently, "Do you have any travel plans lined up?"

Now Cassidy's head jerked around in his direction and she gaped at him, aghast. Even Stella stared at him in surprise. What had Roth found out?

"A trip to Cancun, perhaps? Going solo?"

Cassidy seemed dumbfounded. She looked down at her hands as Roth continued.

"When my team called to say they were bringing you in, I contacted your home number and had a chat to the au pair," Roth explained. "She confirmed that you were not home on the night of the killing, that she did not know your whereabouts at that time, and that you were traveling out of the country this weekend. A last-minute arrangement, I believe. You told her to book yesterday."

Now Cassidy looked outraged. Probably, she'd never dreamed they would find that out, Stella thought. She'd hoped to be safely out of the country by the time the investigation caught up.

"I am not speaking to you anymore!" she stormed. "I refuse to answer any of your questions. I demand my lawyer. You are trying to frame me!"

She clamped her lips shut and folded her arms, glaring at the three of them.

It was incredible, Stella thought. She'd suspected Amanda of being the one with a hidden side, but clearly she'd been wrong. Amanda's big mistake had been making friends with the vicious, false, and reckless Cassidy.

Roth and Maxwell glanced at each other. Then they stepped outside the interview room. Stella followed, closing the door behind them.

"She's not taking us up on the deal. She should be taking us up on the deal. If she's not, it means she was somewhere she doesn't even want us to know. Never mind her husband," Maxwell said in a low voice.

"Could she honestly be that scared of having her husband find out what she was doing?" Stella asked. "Surely, with a murder charge as the alternative, anyone would be willing to talk?"

Unless Cassidy was so egotistical that she thought she could use her lawyer to weasel out of all the charges, Stella thought for a worried moment.

"Look, she already has charges against her for the actions she took earlier. Fleeing confirms that she's got a lot to hide," Roth said.

"She panicked," Stella agreed.

"You were lucky not to be hurt. She was lucky, too," Maxwell said. "That was one crazy ride she took you on. I caught up halfway, for long enough to get good dash cam footage of how she risked your life. It shows how she acts under pressure."

Stella nodded, guessing Maxwell was thinking of what it must have taken to stab Amanda multiple times.

"That ride was terrifying. And yes, her behavior shows that she has a reckless, impulsive personality and that she's prepared to break the law when it suits her."

"When Amanda refused the dare, Cassidy must have thought it was too much of a risk for her," Maxwell suggested.

Cassidy could have arrived at Amanda's home to threaten her further, Stella thought.

"But why was she naked?" Stella wondered.

"Cassidy could have pretended to leave," Maxwell pointed out. "Perhaps Amanda thought she'd won the argument and told Cassidy to get the hell out. But Cassidy was angry, and decided to wait and take revenge instead."

That would make sense, Stella thought. If Cassidy had decided on a plan of action and then rushed upstairs with the knife, that would account for Amanda being naked. Maybe she was getting ready for bed when Cassidy had stormed in.

"You can process her and take her down to the holding cell," Roth told the waiting detective. "She can call her lawyer once she's been processed."

They headed to the back office. Roth was looking satisfied.

"The town council will be pleased that 'a connection' of the victim has been arrested," he said. "A murder committed by a stranger always raises concerns about random crime in the area, which is exactly what they don't want."

"Will the case be strong enough?" Stella asked.

Roth nodded. "Her actions when you approached her, together with her refusal to say where she was on the night of the crime, will build a strong foundation. We can hand over to the local PD now. They can continue with the follow-ups."

"So we just step away?" Stella felt disappointed that they weren't going to see it through all the way to the end.

Maxwell laughed, but she heard a note of sympathy in it.

"Welcome to the real world. I also prefer to have everything neatly in place, but it's now up to the local police department to take the next steps in preparing the case. They'll be the ones managing it from here, not us."

"But—" Stella began. She hated the thought of leaving now.

"That's how it works, because it's not a serial crime, and it was reported to them first," Roth confirmed. "We stayed involved to expedite the investigation and make an arrest, which has now happened. We're still not quite done, though. We have to wrap up from our side."

"How can I help?" Stella asked, wanting to show team spirit.

"I'll give you a job to do. And while we're on the subject of your work, I'm going to write a report for the academy on your conduct during this investigation."

"You are?" Stella asked, feeling nervous. Now she would learn what Roth really thought.

"You were a huge asset to us. You showed resourcefulness, strength of character, professional conduct, ingenuity, courage, and cool logic. All in all, an outstanding young candidate," he praised her.

Stella couldn't believe it. She'd so hoped that she would make a positive impression, after getting off to such a rocky start with this senior agent. She felt proud that she had. Glancing at Maxwell, she was astonished to see him give her a quick, conspiratorial grin. Even Maxwell was pleased!

Then Roth added, "Wherever you're assigned to when you graduate, I know you'll do well."

At the mention of graduation, Stella's happiness evaporated, and in its place, guilty dread loomed. She remembered that Marc would have spent the day following up on Carrie's complaint. Preparing for the worst outcome, she felt sick inside that her own actions might have destroyed her future.

Despite feeling as if her world had ended, Stella did her best to show the qualities Roth had just told her she possessed.

"It's been a privilege to work with both of you. I've learned so much from this investigation and I'll take on board everything you've taught me," she said bravely.

"Let's finish up now," Roth said. "Fall, you can call Maylin, the cleaner. The Gallaghers sent the information through an hour ago, saying that she's now arrived back home in Honduras and has her new phone number organized. Confirm how long she worked for Amanda, and also what time she checked in for her flight, and the flight number. We can include that in the handover. Here's the number. You can work in one of the interview rooms. Ask the front desk for a phone."

Stella headed out of the back office and went to the front desk.

This seemed like a routine fact-check, because the case was all but closed. Even so, Stella wondered whether the cleaner, who had worked so closely with Amanda in her home, might know more about had happened between the two women.

The more evidence that could be piled up against Cassidy, the stronger the case would be.

CHAPTER TWENTY FOUR

Stella headed to the precinct's front desk. Angry shouts resounded from Cassidy's interview room. She could tell the detectives were having a hard time as they began taking her details. Luckily there were other interview rooms further down the corridor that she could use.

"Can I have a phone, please?" she asked.

The desk sergeant handed Stella a phone and she walked to the furthest interview room and closed the door. This would be her last piece of work on the case, and she had to admit, it felt like an anticlimax after the adrenaline rush of bringing Cassidy in, and the tension of that interview with her. But then again, wrapping up a murder investigation for a police handover was valuable experience and she needed to make sure to do it right.

As she dialed Maylin's number, she collected her thoughts and pulled the notebook on the desk toward her.

"*Buenas?*" a woman's voice answered, sounding expectant.

"Hi there. Am I speaking to Maylin?" Stella asked.

"Yes. My name is Maylin Salgado," the woman replied formally.

Although the line was patchy and signal was not great wherever she was, Maylin sounded intelligent and eloquent.

"It's Agent Fall here from the FBI. I'm not sure if the Gallaghers told you about the murder? That Amanda Logan was killed?" Stella assumed that Mrs. Gallagher would have passed on the news, and Maylin's next words confirmed it.

"They called and told me just now. It is terrible! And for it to happen on the same day I left, too, is troubling."

Stella hastened to reassure her.

"The Gallaghers booked you on a flight from JFK that day, so you are not a suspect, but I need you to please confirm the time of the flight."

"It departed at seven p.m. I left the Logans' home an hour early, at twelve noon instead of one, so I could prepare. All my belongings were shipped already. I went home, packed the last few items, and then took a cab straight to the airport. I arrived there at four-thirty p.m. and checked in."

She read out the flight number, which Stella noted down. This information satisfied her that Maylin was cleared and her movements were fully accounted for. Another loose end had been wrapped up.

"You worked for Amanda Logan for how long?"

"For two months, while they were looking for a full-time employee," Maylin said.

Something in her tone alerted Stella.

"Two months is a long time to look," she said.

"The truth is they were very happy with me. There was no need to look. They decided to wait until I left."

"What did you think of Amanda Logan?" Stella asked, feeling curious.

"She was a kind person. She paid me well, tipped me if I did anything extra. She had a temper, though!" Maylin laughed.

"Is that so?" Stella queried.

"Oh, yes. Once or twice when I put things in the wrong place or tidied her personal items so she could not find something, she lost her temper badly. She could shout and scream, that one! She would say I had ruined her life and it would never be the same again. It upset me a few times. I was not used to it."

"Really?" Stella asked, feeling concerned.

"Then, five minutes later, she would be back to normal, as sweet and kind as ever. Apologizing over and over for what she'd done. She told me she was trying hard to be a better person, and that she hated to lose her temper with anyone."

"Did she lose her temper in the last few days?" Stella asked, wondering if Amanda would have shown any reaction after Cassidy's dare.

"Yes. She came back very angry after a get-together with her friends. She was crying. She went into the kitchen and threw a plate all the way across the room. I asked her what was wrong, but she refused to say. She went and shut herself away in her room for a while, which was very unusual for her. I felt so bad for her that I even mentioned it to Mrs. Gallagher. I thought she must have had a serious fight."

"Did she ever tell you any details?" Stella asked.

"No. She didn't say anything more about it. I hardly saw her after that. She was out a lot of the time," Maylin said. "I saw her on the morning of the last day I worked. She looked happy, as if things were going well for her again. I remember thinking that whatever had been wrong, she must have sorted it out. She thanked me and gave me a bonus."

"I really appreciate you telling me this," Stella said. "Thank you for your time."

She put the phone down feeling unsure all over again. She stared around the bland interview room with its one-way glass and blank walls, thinking of the insights she'd just received.

Maylin had confirmed Amanda's hidden side. The sweet, kind woman everyone was describing had a terrible temper. And from what Maylin had said, she'd been very upset by Cassidy's ultimatum. What did that mean? What had she done?

Had she confronted Cassidy and threatened her? Stella wondered. It seemed possible, since both women were impulsive. A vicious fight could have ended with Cassidy deciding to silence her once and for all.

Even though the details might never be known, she was sure that Roth would be pleased with this interview that helped to wrap up the case.

She left the interview room and went to return the phone. At the front desk, Stella saw Cassidy was once again causing a minor commotion. She'd found her voice again and was shouting angrily. Detective Grant looked nervous as he removed her handcuff to allow her to sign the final documents.

"Other one. I use the other one," Cassidy said in angry tones, and the detective hastily complied.

Stella watched for a moment, relieved that she was now under formal arrest. She hoped that there would be enough evidence for the charges to hold up, that the jury would be convinced of her guilt, and that Cassidy wasn't keeping information back.

She still felt a creeping sense of fear that Cassidy had in fact been out on a dare, but that she was waiting for her lawyer's advice before giving an alibi to prove she had an innocent reason for being where she was.

If that happened, the whole case would crumble and then where would they be?

Firmly, Stella told herself not to overthink. They had a strong suspect in custody and the rest would be up to the local police.

"Ma'am! Wait!" Detective Grant sounded panicked.

In typical form, once she'd signed the papers, Cassidy turned and hurled the pen across the police station. It ricocheted off the wall near the entrance door.

"Enough of that!" he said angrily.

She'd earned her handcuffs again. Detective Grant snapped them back onto her wrists and hustled her through the door that led to the holding cells, looking thoroughly fed up with her behavior.

It would all count against her, Stella hoped. But then, with a cold shock, she realized what she had been looking at.

Right in front of her was a crucial detail she'd missed. They'd all missed it.

"Oh no," she whispered.

Cassidy could not have been the killer. She could not! Despite her behavior, and all the circumstantial evidence, someone else must have committed the crime.

Stella rushed through to the back office where Maxwell and Roth were seated at opposite sides of the large desk, both typing furiously on their laptops.

"Interview went well?" Roth inquired, looking up.

"She couldn't have done it, Roth. Cassidy could not have killed Amanda!" Stella stated.

Now Maxwell looked up too, frowning. Roth sighed.

"We're wrapping things up. Concluding our case." He emphasized the word "concluding." "This is not the moment for random theories. Did the cleaner give you any evidence of anyone else being involved?"

He asked the question in a way that told her he was trying to be patient but that he was sure the cleaner had not.

"She said Amanda was very upset after it happened. But that's not why I believe Cassidy's not guilty."

"Why is that?" Roth rubbed his fingers over his forehead as if a headache was starting.

"I watched her signing the forms for her charges when I returned the phone."

"What did you notice?" Now Roth was looking worried.

"Cassidy is left-handed. She signed all the documents with her left hand. I watched her do it. Then she threw the pen across the room, also with her left hand. Without a doubt, she's left-dominant."

"Are you sure?" Roth asked, but he sounded as if he was clutching at straws.

"Very sure. Detective Grant automatically took her right hand out of the cuffs, and she started yelling at him that she used the other one. She had to have her left hand freed before she could write with the pen. Her lawyer will pick up on that as soon as he sees the postmortem results. The jury will agree. She'll be cleared of the crime and will walk free. She probably won't even have to go into detail about her whereabouts on the night. And in any case, she obviously didn't do it!" Stella further pleaded. "Why would she hold a knife in her weaker hand when she needed to put all her force into the killing blows? It must have been someone else."

CHAPTER TWENTY FIVE

Maxwell swore, burying his head in his hands as Stella watched sympathetically. That was how she felt, too.

Roth pressed his lips together. Then he gave a reluctant nod.

"You're correct. It's going to be a major flaw in the case. But we don't have an alternative suspect."

"I had a thought about that," Stella said.

"Explain to me, Fall," Roth said.

"The only other explanation is that Amanda went ahead with the dare and she was somehow murdered as a result. I wondered earlier if she had done it, and I went to her house to see if I could find any evidence of trophies. Then Maxwell called to say he knew where Cassidy was, so I left in a hurry. After everything that happened with Cassidy, we didn't pursue that line of thought."

She thought again of Amanda being naked. It did point to a dare. It did! Something had gone wrong and Amanda had been killed instead.

"There's no evidence of her organizing a meet-up," Roth emphasized.

"There might be. I found a little booklet in her vanity drawer, with initials and dates written inside. It's worth trying to find out what they are. When Cassidy was arrested I didn't think the booklet would be important, but now I'd like to check it out. Do you have the list of Amanda's calls for the past few months? I'd like to compare the list with the booklet and see if anything matches up."

"In the file there, there's a hard copy of her calls." He pointed.

"May I take it with me to the interview room?"

Stella held her breath waiting for Roth to decide.

"Go ahead. Remember, it's confidential information and we need this wrapped up fast. So if you have a theory, it needs to be provable."

Stella hurried back to the interview room with the pages in her hand. Closing the door, she set out the sheets. Then, with hope simmering inside her, she took the little black book, with its scrawled dates and initials, out of her bag.

Would anything add up? Did this book have any significance?

As she paged through the book, Stella noticed something strange. There were about seven entries there, but all the dates except for one were for earlier in the year, while Amanda was still in Hastings and before she moved to Fairfield.

However, the final date in the book was the day after Cassidy had given her that fateful dare and Stella felt a renewed determination as she picked up on this fact.

Would these dates and initials correspond at all with the list of calls? Roth had checked the numbers out, but hadn't gone into detail beyond that. Stella was going to go into detail. She was going to try and find out what had been said in those calls.

She realized immediately that every date in the black book corresponded with a call. Thanks to Roth's thorough work, it was possible to pair up a few of the initials in the book with the calls that had been made.

Carefully, Stella scanned through the list.

FD on May twentieth. That matched up to Ferdinand Donald: Realtor, in the call log. Amanda had called him on the morning of the twentieth. Roth had noted Ferdinand Donald was a real estate agent. Perhaps they'd already been looking to sell their home in Hastings at that point. Or perhaps not.

Stella called the number, feeling nerves jitter inside her. This felt so important, as if she was on the verge of a breakthrough.

"Hello?" a deep, rather impatient voice said.

"Is this Mr. Donald?" Stella asked.

"It is. I'm in a meeting so make it quick."

"I'm Stella Fall, calling from the FBI. It's in connection with the murder of Amanda Logan."

"Yes?" Now his voice was filled with suspicion.

"You're not in any trouble. We were just trying to ascertain your relationship to the victim?"

"I valued their house," Donald snapped.

"Were you friends with Mrs. Logan at all, outside of business?"

There was a short pause.

"What are you implying?" he asked again, sounding angry. "I told you. I valued their house. I have no more to say."

He paused for a moment, as if weighing up the wisdom of putting the phone down on the FBI. Then, decision clearly made, the line went dead.

Stella felt all her instincts prickle. Mr. Donald had been way too defensive. There was more to this, she was sure. But it wasn't going to be easy to get the information, as his response had proved. She needed to get her thoughts in order and work on her approach to these contacts.

She checked the list, working back. Here was a name on March first that tied into the initials TK. Ted Knight. Roth had noted that he ran TK Catering.

Feeling curious, and wanting as much information as possible, she checked out the company online before calling.

The web page brought up a head and shoulders photo of a handsome, roguishly smiling, dark-haired man who was probably forty years old.

"Hi, I'm Ted of TK Catering, and my team and I are ready to fulfill all your foodie fantasies!" the tagline read.

Okay, Stella thought. Ted was the right age, he was good-looking, and clearly, from the double entendre in the tagline, Ted was an adventurous person. But how adventurous had he been with Amanda? Was this what this little black book was all about?

She felt stunned to think that Amanda might have been doing meet-ups with men long before the time she even met the three Fairfield friends. It was bizarre, but this was what it was starting to look like. That raised a whole lot more questions; chief among them why she was so offended by Cassidy's dare. Was it because Cassidy had tried to force her?

For now, she needed proof that this had in fact happened, and for one person at least to confirm her theory. Roth would demand proof.

Feeling extremely nervous now, and under pressure of time, Stella called Ted's number.

He didn't answer. It rang through to voicemail and she let out a disappointed breath.

Time to move on to the next one on the list. On February fifth, DD appeared in the little black book. That matched up to Donovan Dunning, who according to the list, owned Don's Depot. Stella couldn't tell from the name what kind of company it was. She guessed something to do with storage, but there were no notes to say if Amanda had used it.

She called the number and Donovan answered on the first ring. He sounded as if he was driving.

"Hi, Don here."

"Hello. I'm Stella Fall. I'm assisting with an FBI investigation into the murder of Amanda Logan. I believe you knew Mrs. Logan?"

"I'm sorry. I'm driving. I'm unable to take your call now," Don said quickly, with a note of panic in his voice. Before Stella had uttered another word, or was able to tell him to wait, he cut the call.

She sighed. He hadn't sounded worried about driving until he'd found out who Stella was and she'd mentioned Amanda's name. She was getting the sense that all the men knew something, but nobody was saying anything.

Face to face would be so much easier, but going all the way to Hastings to track down someone who was willing to talk would be impossible right now.

She turned back to her list, but was interrupted by her phone ringing.

"Hello?" she answered, and to her surprise, found herself speaking to a friendly-sounding man with a British accent.

"It's Ted here from TK Catering. Sorry I missed your call."

Stella suppressed the thought that he was probably going to be even sorrier that he'd returned it. Although Ted sounded friendlier than the others had. Perhaps he would be outspoken enough to admit what had happened.

"Mr. Knight, I'm Agent Fall, assisting with an FBI investigation into Amanda Logan's death," she began.

"Ah, yes. I heard about that," Ted said, sounding intrigued. "Terrible thing to happen."

She thought he was about to say something else, but then he didn't. The silence sounded expectant.

"I'm trying to tie up some details. You are not a suspect. However, I am looking into Amanda's private life, hoping that I can better understand her past activities."

"Go on?" Ted said. He sounded mildly amused, rather than defensive. Stella felt a rush of encouragement.

"Your initials were in what I can only describe as a little black book," Stella said.

"They were?" Now Ted sounded surprised.

"Do you know why?"

Ted sighed. "It sounds as if you already know—or at any rate, that you've guessed," he admitted.

"I'm seeking confirmation of the facts," she encouraged him.

Ted paused. Sounding cautious, he continued.

"I assume this is an off-the-record chat? I'd hate to find what I said plastered all over tomorrow's headlines," he warned. "Can I have your assurance of that please?"

"It's for background only, and off the record. What we discuss will remain confidential," Stella reassured him.

"Well, the lovely Mrs. Logan and I shared a gym. A new gym opened in town, and we met there—we both worked out at similar times. It wasn't long before things got rather flirty between us. From her side, you understand. I was uneasy about overstepping the line with an obviously married woman. When I'm in a relationship, I don't cheat. But Mrs. Logan had absolutely no hesitation about leaping over that line and seemed not to care about the fact she was married at all. In rather a short time, she suggested a get-together."

Goose bumps chased themselves up and down Stella's spine. This was exactly the modus operandi that the friends had used. But Amanda had clearly been doing it long before she met them.

"What was your reaction?"

"I agreed, of course. I had the sense she wasn't looking for everlasting love," Ted quipped. "I thought perhaps she was a bored wife looking for adventure, or that she had an open relationship. We had two very passionate assignations in the space of a week, and after that, she changed her time at the gym and never contacted me again." He hesitated, as if about to say something else.

"Go on?" Stella said.

"What I wanted to say was that as much as I enjoyed our little sessions, I did feel worried for her. It was—well, I am not one to dictate to others how they live their lives. But such behavior is reckless. In that situation, not everybody will respond the way you expect them to. And a woman is always more at risk. It shouldn't be so, but it is. So honestly, Agent Fall, I was sad when I heard she had been killed, but I was not surprised. If she continued with this behavior, it struck me that it might have led to her death."

Stella felt stunned by this information.

"You've been so helpful. I appreciate your honesty."

"That's me," Ted laughed. "Honest Ted. I hope you catch the killer."

"I'll do my best," Stella promised.

She put the phone down.

So Amanda had done exactly the same as her friends. She'd cheated—deliberately and systematically. Why had she done such a thing? Stella wondered, feeling shattered by the destructiveness of her behavior.

With her heart in her mouth, she checked the black book again. Now the last entry in that book, the day after the dare, seemed even more important. This was clear evidence that Amanda had cheated again. Given the timing, it meant she'd taken Cassidy up on her challenge, and then something had gone horribly wrong.

The initials were OC. Who was OC? With hands now shaking with excitement, Stella checked the call records.

And let out a frustrated sigh.

There were more than ten calls on the record for that day. Amanda had called her husband at the office. Perhaps that had been to check he wasn't going to be home. Then she'd called the beauty salon, and an art dealer, two courier companies, a carpet cleaner, the local nursery, and a shelving company. She'd called her car insurance, and a few other insurance companies, too. Perhaps she'd been looking to get quotes for the contents of her new home. She'd then called two clothing boutiques and a local deli. None of the businesses, at first glance, matched up with the initials she needed. She'd have to contact every business, and ask them the surprising question of whether they had anyone working for them with those initials.

It would take a long time, and some of the businesses would have many employees. Finding the information could take days.

Or maybe there was a quicker way, Stella thought

There was one person who might know who OC was, because Amanda might have mentioned the name innocently in passing. That person was her husband.

Stella hurried back to the precinct's back office, where Roth looked up inquiringly.

"Well?" he asked. "What information did you find?"

Taking a deep breath, Stella explained the back story.

"Amanda was doing exactly the same as the three friends. Before she even met them."

"What do you mean?" The sharpness in Roth's eyes told her that he did, in fact, guess what she meant, but needed her to say it.

"She cheated with random men. She had a little black book where she wrote down dates and initials. I spoke to one of her lovers back in Hastings who confirmed it. She had the technique down pat. She'd flirt, hook them in, organize a meet-up, and then ghost them. The man I spoke to mentioned that it was dangerous behavior. That he wasn't surprised when he heard she was murdered."

Roth pressed his lips together. Stella could see he was thinking hard.

"So her cheating behavior continued here?" Maxwell asked incredulously.

"It stopped at first. I have a feeling she tried to put it behind her. Turn over a new leaf with the move, you know? But then, the day after Cassidy's dare, she wrote another set of initials in the book. OC. So it looks like she took the dare."

Stella handed the book to Roth. He paged through, frowning down.

"If Cassidy didn't kill Amanda, it had to be OC. But she made so many calls the day before the meet-up that it's not possible to see who OC is at a glance. None of the business names match up, and she called a few big companies who'll have hundreds of people working for them."

"All the calls I checked seemed routine, and there were no suspicious messages in the logs," Roth agreed.

"So I've had a thought. Perhaps Craig knows. Amanda might have mentioned OC innocently, in conversation. He might know who this person is."

Roth nodded. "All right. You want to go speak to Craig?"

"Yes, I do."

"You know where he is?"

"Detective Grant said he was staying at the Marriott. Can I meet him there?" Stella asked.

"Yes. I'm going to call him now and ask him to meet you in the hotel lounge. And meanwhile, Maxwell and I will try and think of any other angles we've missed that could lead to his identity."

"Thank you," Stella said gratefully.

She had one chance now. One last chance to discover who Amanda's killer was. But as she climbed in her car, she couldn't help feeling a shiver of fear that OC, whoever he was, might never be found.

CHAPTER TWENTY SIX

Half an hour later, Stella arrived at the Marriott. Her stomach felt taut with tension as she headed inside.

She saw Craig there immediately. He was seated at a table in the corner with two laptops open in front of him. Clearly, despite his compassionate leave from the office, he was immersing himself in work as a coping mechanism.

Quickly, she headed over to the table, making her way through the quiet, coffee-scented lounge that at this time was mostly empty. When Craig saw her he stood up and closed both the lids. He looked more coherent than he had been the last time she'd seen him, although he was still very pale and seemed gaunt, as if he'd been forgetting to eat.

"I'm catching up on work. It's a distraction, but at least it keeps my mind off everything. Why are you here?" he asked her. "Detective Grant called me earlier to say a suspect had been arrested. It was one of Amanda's girlfriends, he said."

"Yes. Someone is in custody. And yes, it's one of Amanda's girlfriends. However, I'm following up on a few details and need to confirm something with you."

"What details?" Craig said. Then, as if remembering his manners too late, he added, "Please sit."

Stella sat opposite, and Craig resumed his place in front of the now-closed laptops. He stared at her, tapping his fingers on one of the lids.

Gathering her thoughts, Stella planned how she was going to approach it. It was a desperately sensitive topic. Only now, sitting in front of him, did she fully realize the enormity of what she was doing.

Up until now, Craig Logan likely had no idea that Amanda was a cheater. Stella would be responsible for tainting his memories of his wife forever.

She wished she didn't have to do this, but if she didn't, then the person who murdered his wife might never be found. It was a horrific trade-off. She hoped that given the choice, Craig would rather see justice done. Taking a deep breath, she began to speak.

"This is not easy to say," Stella broached the topic in a gentle voice. "Craig, I've recently learned that your wife had a different side to her."

As she spoke, she watched him carefully. Did he suspect she had done this? Or was this totally new information?

"The three friends that she met for bridge games weren't really into bridge at all. Their sessions were a chance to dare each other to cheat. And at their last get-together, about a week ago, Amanda was dared, too."

"To cheat?" Now she heard tension in his voice. He laced his fingers tightly together. "Amanda? I—she surely wouldn't have done such a thing. I have no idea about her friends, or what kind of people they are," he added emphatically.

"Did you ever see this book anywhere?"

Stella took it out of her purse and held it out to him. He looked down at it. She flipped slowly through the pages, allowing him a look at the dates and initials in his wife's handwriting.

Watching his face closely, Stella saw he didn't seem shocked. Instead, he appeared expressionless. She had the sense he was thinking hard.

"What are these? What's this book all about? I might have seen it before, but I can't remember where. Where was it?"

"It was in her vanity drawer," she said.

"I didn't ever go through her personal stuff." He sounded defensive now. "What is the reason you're showing it to me?" he added.

"It's a book of appointments," she told him, even though she was sure he must now already suspect this.

"What are you saying? Stop—stop hinting at things!"

His tone was furious now. Craig was all out of patience with her subtle approach. It was time to spit out the truth.

"Craig, I hate to have to tell you this. I'm feeling terrible sitting here in front of you, knowing that I have to share this information with you. But it's crucial to the case. Do you understand?"

He gave a small nod.

Stella continued. "There are dates and initials in the book that go back to before you moved here. There are dates right back to last year, when you lived in Hastings. From time to time, Amanda was hooking up with random guys and sleeping with them. I'm really sorry that she felt the need to do this. But perhaps you guessed there was a different side to her?" Stella asked, hoping that he wouldn't completely shut down, or freak out and ask her to leave, now that she had delivered her bombshell.

He stared at her in raw despair.

"I can't believe this," Craig whispered.

He dropped his head into his hands, but then raised it again, so suddenly that she jumped.

"Prove it!" he challenged her. "Prove this to me!"

Stella sensed that his emotions were balanced on a knife edge. She worried that he might try to snatch the book from her and tear it up or otherwise destroy it.

Being careful to keep a firm hold on the little book, she paged through it.

"On the twentieth of May, were you home? Did Amanda mention going out anywhere? At that stage she was still working part time, if I recall?"

"The twentieth of May?" Now Craig sounded defensive, as if there was no way he could remember that particular date from any other.

"Do you have a diary? Perhaps you can look up the date," Stella prompted.

"A—yes, I do. I can look it up here."

Impatiently, he tapped computer keys.

"That was our annual work conference. I was away for the night. Not far from home, we were in a hotel an hour away."

"Amanda organized a meet-up with someone on that date," Stella told him.

Craig stared at her in silence. He'd shut down and she couldn't tell what he was thinking. His face was like stone.

"What about March first?" she then said.

"March first?" Again, Craig tapped keys. "She was at a bachelorette party all day. She got back very late."

Stella shook her head. "She wasn't at a bachelorette party. She was meeting someone with the initials TK, who was Ted Knight, from the phone records."

Turning the book to him, she showed him the scrawled date and initials.

He said nothing but stared at it in silence. The tension was so tight in the spacious lounge that Stella felt as if the air itself might crack.

Then his face tautened and Stella knew he'd reached snapping point.

He jumped to his feet and grabbed the carafe of water on the table. Stella ducked, cringing away as he flung it down. It smashed on the polished floorboards, water splashing everywhere.

"I do not believe this," he yelled. "I don't believe you are here telling me this. How evil and immoral do you have to be? Why are you even doing this to me? Why, why, why? Won't you let me remember her the way I want her to be? You are a poisonous, terrible person!"

Concerned cries erupted from the guests at the far side of the lounge.

"It's all okay," Stella said, raising her voice as she turned to them with a reassuring smile. "Just an accident. Could a waiter pick up the glass, please?"

Turning back to Craig, she summoned all the calm energy she could find.

"Please understand, she had stopped doing it. She stopped when you moved to Fairfield. She put her old ways behind her, but then Cassidy challenged her. Amanda was furious about it. I don't think she would have done it to be accepted back into the group of friends. That doesn't seem to align with who Amanda was. My guess is that she intended it to be a form of revenge, or payback, somehow. And then something went wrong. This person must have killed her. That's why I'm sitting here in front of you now. You need to accept this happened, and try to help me."

All the rage deflated from Craig. He seemed to shrink before her eyes.

Stella realized that the waiter had arrived and was bustling around, picking up the cracked carafe and mopping the water.

"Thank you so much." Stella smiled again.

When the waiter had left, Craig slumped into his chair and stared at her, looking broken.

"Did you know what she was doing?" Stella asked softly.

He shook his head. "I didn't know. But I can't say that I didn't have moments when I wondered. She was such a beautiful person, but there was another side to her also. She had a secret side, and she was very defensive about keeping some things private."

"Did you ever suspect she was cheating?"

"Yes, there were times when I wondered, at the back of my mind, if she might be. You see, I knew she was a free spirit. She was dating someone else when we met. She broke it off with him, but then there was a—an episode—when I suspected she'd changed her mind and gone back to him. I was in love and desperately wanted things to work out. In fact, I was in denial," he said sadly.

"What about when you moved here?" Stella asked.

"With the new job and the move, I hoped that the money and the house would make everything okay. We both agreed what an amazing opportunity this was, and that we could make a fresh start here, that it was time for us to have a family. Deep down, I hoped that she'd changed and finally gotten over her wild behavior. And you say she had. Until this happened."

"Do the initials OC mean anything to you? Those are the last initials in the book and, as you can see, the date is just after the get-together with her friends. Do you have any idea who OC is? Can you recall her mentioning anyone with a first name beginning with O?" she asked.

Craig shook his head again, helplessly. "I wish I could answer. I don't know a thing. I was working so hard this past week."

"I'm sorry," Stella sympathized. She felt terrible to have been the messenger who had brought Craig this bad news.

Craig stared at her, his eyes reddened.

"How do you ever learn to trust again after something like this has happened? How do I trust again?"

His words burned Stella. She remembered how it had ended with her own fiancé, how he'd changed in front of her eyes, how she'd gradually realized what was in his history, and how she'd been helpless to stop the train smash of events from occurring.

"I don't know, Mr. Logan. All I can say is that I also hope it's possible, after something like this," she said.

"Find him. Whoever he was, find him. I want him locked away for life," Craig said, and there was a viciousness in his tone she'd never heard before.

"Where can I look?" Stella pleaded. "Where would your wife have kept something private, that she didn't want you to see?"

Craig buried his face in his hands and for a while, she thought he wasn't going to answer. Then, finally, he raised his head.

"Did you check her car?" he asked thoughtfully. "It's the only place I can think of. She was careless about taking stuff out of it. Her car was a mess, and she used to get angry when I asked her to clean it out or take it for a valet polish. It was her private space, I decided." He gave a haunted smile.

Stella felt her heart accelerate. She hadn't checked the car. Nobody had. Until an hour ago, there had been no reason to do so, but now there was.

“I’ll check the car. That’s a very good suggestion. Thank you so much for your help.”

She got up and walked quietly out of the lobby.

Then, with hope and anxiety warring inside her at the last-chance idea Craig had provided, she headed purposefully to the Logans’ house.

CHAPTER TWENTY SEVEN

At the Logans' house, Stella opened the front door and then hurried through the house until she reached the garage's side door. She felt breathless with expectancy that the clue she was seeking might be hidden here. She was determined to find something that pointed to OC's identity.

Stepping inside, she saw the garage was a quiet, tidy space. Uncluttered. The only items in it were a gold Lexus, a few steel storage chests, and a gleaming mountain bike which Stella guessed belonged to Craig and which hadn't been used much.

Stella opened the car door and the light shone onto the leather-scented space.

She drew in her breath. Craig was right. The car was not as neat as the garage, and Amanda had clearly been careless about leaving her possessions inside. There was a lime green sweater and a silver scarf carelessly thrown onto the back seat, and below the passenger seat, she saw a pair of high-heeled silver shoes. Presumably they were uncomfortable to drive in and she had kicked them off and left them there. There were discarded mint wrappers in the central console and an empty water bottle in one of the cup holders. A pair of sunglasses was stashed near the gearstick, together with a lipstick, a nail file, and a few diamante hairclips.

None of these looked like a potential trophy and all of them looked like Amanda's own personal possessions.

Stella explored further, opening the leather-covered compartment between the seats and checking inside. There, she found another empty water bottle, lip balm, eyebrow tweezers, three more lipsticks, and a crumpled Kleenex.

None of these were right either. She didn't know what she was looking for but it wasn't ordinary paraphernalia. She needed a handwritten note, a map, or better still, something that could provide evidence of OC himself.

She gritted her teeth in frustration that nothing like this seemed to be so conveniently available.

The only thing in the cubbyhole was the car's manual. Stella checked the carpets, peered under the seats. Nothing. Perhaps there was nothing to be found. Feeling devastated, she accepted this possibility. At any rate, she'd tried.

It was almost by accident that she slipped her hand into one of the silver shoes and felt something cool, small, and solid in the toe.

Curiously, Stella shook the object out.

It was a cufflink, made from gold and bright blue lapis lazuli. It was clearly an expensive antique, with a marquis crest pressed into the stone. And on the other side, it had been engraved with an initial—the letter O.

Stella drew in her breath as she stared at it, touching the finely crafted item with shaking fingers.

This was what she needed. It was undoubtedly a trophy. It had to be! There was no other reason for its presence here in the car, hidden away in Amanda's shoe. It must belong to OC. It must!

Who, who, who could he possibly be? What was the significance of this fine, antique item and how could she trace it back to him?

Stella frantically puzzled over the possibilities. Sitting in the plush leather-lined car, she turned all her focus to potential scenarios, sensing the irony that she was doing so amid the last few traces of Amanda's personal life. She remembered what had played out at that get-together when Amanda had been dared, and how upset she had been.

Someone so angry would not just have accepted the dare, Stella suddenly thought. She would have wanted more. A secret, Stella realized. That was the hidden side of Amanda, the side Craig had just told her about. She needed her secrets.

How did this expensive piece of men's jewelry tie in with those desires?

And as she sat there, holding the cufflink, it suddenly came to her, so blindingly obvious that she grabbed the wheel, clutching the soft leather tightly.

Of course! Of course!

Chills constricted her spine. She knew the significance of this trophy and why Amanda had chosen it. She knew who OC was. The only thing she didn't know was why Amanda had done it.

This was beyond revenge. It seemed the most destructive action she could have taken, in every way, and Stella couldn't fathom it.

There was only one person who could provide reasons for Amanda's actions, and that was OC himself.

Every second counted now. She needed to confront him with the truth, as soon as possible. He was a wealthy man with infinite resources at his disposal. She feared he might already have guessed they were onto him, and made plans to flee while he could.

*

Ten minutes later, Stella pulled up outside the luxury mansion.

She shivered, feeling a gust of cold wind rattle the leaves of the gracious oak tree in the finely kept yard. Her fingers felt icy as she lifted them to ring the bell.

Would anyone be home?

The only sound was her heart, pounding loudly in her ears. Perhaps nobody would be home; her insight could have come too late.

Her mouth felt dry as she wondered how long she should wait before ringing the bell again. Then she stopped breathing completely as she heard soft footsteps approach.

Someone was here.

The door opened and she came face to face with the man she wanted.

Stella struggled to remain calm, and to keep her face from showing any of the emotion that was now boiling side her.

He must have just gotten back from work, and was smartly dressed in a gray cashmere coat over a suit and tie. He was a tall, handsome man. She immediately noticed his dark good looks and those expensive clothes.

"Good evening," he said, looking surprised. "Who are you?"

"Good evening, Mr. Cooper. I'm FBI Agent Fall," Stella told him. "I came by hoping to speak to you quickly."

Now, he looked harassed. "Is it important? I don't have much time. I'm packaging a meal for my wife and then I'm heading straight over to the police station to drop this off. Our lawyer's on his way, but they are refusing to release her tonight, and she only eats a plant-based diet. The police said I could bring her something."

As he spoke, Stella realized that the house was silent. The au pair must have taken Cassidy's children to family. Her spine prickled as she guessed this meant that he, too, was planning to leave. The words "drop this off" were a tell. Why would he just drop a package and run? Why wouldn't he stay and meet with the lawyer?

"Kayla's just taken the kids to their aunt. They're staying there a few days." Mr. Cooper words worsened her suspicions.

As she stood in the hall, she took another look around. As she had been on her first visit, she was impressed by the variety of paintings on the walls, the Indonesian wall hangings, the magnificent prayer mat on the floor, and the hall table, which she guessed was a lovingly maintained and highly expensive antique piece.

And, worst of all, she noticed a large black valise, standing under the hall table.

He must have realized that as soon as his wife was cleared, the police would continue their hunt.

Mr. Cooper turned and hurried through to the kitchen. Stella followed him. There, he took a cardboard container from out of the fridge and placed it in a bag.

In contrast to the rest of the house, so rich in historical items, the kitchen was brightly lit and modern. Silver gleamed everywhere—from the massive, double-door refrigerator to the gleaming stove hob to the chrome appliances. What wasn't silver was black—granite countertops, dark matte blinds, ebony cupboards and drawers.

"I won't take much of your time, Mr. Cooper. I came here to check up on a few details regarding the case." Somehow, she had to delay him. She had to get the information she needed so that they could make an arrest.

"Please, call me Oliver," he invited her, as her stomach twisted so violently it felt painful.

Oliver stared down at the bag thoughtfully, and then at Stella again for a long moment. "Shall we speak in the study?" he asked.

Stella felt glad to get out of the kitchen. She'd noticed a block of sharp knives on one of the counters. The study felt like a safer place to be face-to-face with Amanda's killer. But did he know that she knew? From his face, she didn't think so, but he had a hard face to read.

"I'm extremely anxious about my wife. She's been wrongfully arrested and is a victim in all of this," Oliver told her as they headed up a wide staircase.

"You don't think she's the killer?" Stella asked.

"Of course not. We all know how the police can twist things to suit themselves. Having this case unsolved is damaging their reputation. Cassidy could say something in innocence that would be held against her. Her lawyer advised her to wait until he could consult with her and get everything factually correct."

"That's good advice."

He glanced at her, frowning. "Are you here to try and collect more evidence? What exactly are you needing from me?"

Oliver stopped outside a wooden door, opened it, and snapped on the light. It glowed over oak-paneled walls and an enormous desk.

Then he stood back, allowing Stella to go in first. He gestured to one of the plush, leather-upholstered armchairs by the bookcase in the far corner, and took a seat in the other.

"I wanted to confirm that you are in the art and antiques supply business, Oliver. I remember your wife mentioned it the first time we interviewed her. The décor in your home is incredible," Stella praised. She hoped she sounded normal. Her mouth felt dry and her heart was pounding.

Oliver frowned at her, clearly confused by her words.

"You didn't come here to admire the décor, did you?" he snapped. "If you need to confirm my profession, then yes. I'm a dealer in fine art and antiques. I don't see how that's relevant. Are you done now? This is a stressful time for us, and I'm in a hurry."

Panic surged inside her. She couldn't let him leave. She doubted he would even go past the police station, now that he was so suspicious. Instead, she worried he would drive straight to the airport and jump on a plane, and it would be too late. She had to force him to confirm the facts of what he'd done.

Stella decided it was time to spill out the truth.

"Amanda Logan called your art dealership last week. I saw it noted on the list of calls, but didn't immediately realize it was connected to you. She obviously must have asked for you personally. You already knew who she was, of course. The charming, beautiful woman that you'd met a few times in passing, during Cassidy's social events?"

Now Oliver's face looked very still.

"I don't think it was just a social call and I don't think she wanted art, although perhaps she did make a private appointment with you. But the purpose of her call was to organize a meet-up with you. A seduction. At some stage in the next day or two, you slept with Amanda," Stella said.

"That's a crazy claim to make. It's both insulting and completely false. Why would I ever do such a thing?" Oliver asked, sounding outraged.

"I'm sure it was in a reckless moment. She's very beautiful. And, although you don't know this, she's also extremely practiced in seduction. You probably didn't stand a chance once she had her sights set on you. It might have felt as if you were watching it happen to someone else," Stella suggested.

Oliver shook his head adamantly, regarding her in silence. Stella pressed on, looking for the moment when he might crack.

"You must have soon realized that one of your cufflinks was missing. They look like very special items and pieces that you couldn't risk losing. Being antiques, you also could not easily replace a missing one. Perhaps Cassidy even gave them to you?"

Now Stella saw the truth of it in his face, almost imperceptibly. His gaze darted left and right. His mouth tightened briefly. For a moment he seemed to be fighting to regain his steely control.

"So, my theory is that you then returned to the Logans' house, probably after confirming with Amanda that she would, in fact, be alone that night. You asked for your cufflink but she refused to give it to you. You knew that this refusal represented a serious threat to you and your marriage, because why would she not hand it innocently back?"

Again, she saw the truth of it in the twitching of his face, the narrowing of his eyes.

And, suddenly, Stella realized what Amanda must have planned.

She was never going to show the trophy to Cassidy. Of course not. That would have put Amanda's marriage at risk as well. That wasn't how her mind worked. She didn't tell anyone her private thoughts.

She would have been happy to keep her revenge a secret, to stash the cufflink somewhere and know that those initials were noted in the little black book. She'd have ghosted the trio of friends, just as she'd done with others in the past.

And she would have gloated alone in the knowledge that she'd gotten the ultimate revenge.

Now Stella could imagine how the scene might have played out.

"I'm guessing she teased you. She wouldn't give you a straight answer. Perhaps she giggled and evaded the question and said why wouldn't you let her keep a little gift? And perhaps she reassured you that it was only her secret and she would never tell anyone, particularly your wife."

From the way Oliver gave an almost imperceptible flinch, Stella guessed she was correct.

"You didn't believe her, though, because you knew she was friends with Cassidy. And as she argued and refused, you got more and more scared. Her confidence made you feel terrified. Your fears started to run away with you and you realized how reckless and stupid your actions had been, and what it could cost you. So, finally, you decided that there was only one way to handle this, which was to make sure she could never, ever tell on you."

Still, Oliver stared at her in silence. His body language was betraying him, but he wasn't saying a word.

She knew she was right, that she was pressing buttons, that she was pushing him toward the breaking point. But he hadn't broken! At some point, surely, the stress would force him to.

Determinedly, she continued.

"You felt desperate. Perhaps you were in the kitchen at the time. She might have been finishing off her wine." Stella could picture Amanda's cool composure and how she must have laughed at Oliver's frantic pleas.

"You quickly made your plan. You pretended it didn't matter, and said she could keep the cufflink. And explained your real reason for visiting her had been to sleep with her again. And, because by then she was a little drunk, she was stupid enough to believe you," Stella said. What a misjudgment that had been on Amanda's part.

She paused, wondering what to say next. She'd been certain that Oliver would break, and would confess to what he'd done. But he hadn't. He'd held his nerve, even though she'd guessed this account would have tipped him over the edge.

Her judgment of him had been incorrect. And then, yet again, Oliver Cooper surprised her.

"Stand up, please. Before I leave, I want to show you something important," he said.

Feeling shaken, Stella stood. What did he want to show her? She felt she was losing control. How could she guide this conversation where she needed it to go?

Oliver quickly moved a few paces away from her, toward the door.

And then, her heart accelerated as she saw him take a silver pistol from a holster that had been concealed under his coat. She hadn't noticed it. She hadn't even considered that he would be carrying and her attention had been focused elsewhere. At this critical time, she'd made a lethal mistake.

The metallic click signaled he was removing the gun's safety catch.

CHAPTER TWENTY EIGHT

"Amanda did believe me when I said I wanted to sleep with her again," Oliver told Stella in a surprisingly calm tone as he aimed the pistol at her chest. "It all played out much as you described."

Stella stared at him in horror. He was holding her at gunpoint! This was never the way she thought she'd get her confession. Numbly, she listened to him, even as her mind raced frantically ahead, panicking over how she could save herself.

"I took a knife from the block. I followed her upstairs. I knew I was going to have to use it on her because everything was at stake. Everything. My life. My business, which Cassidy co-owns and funded. Our marriage. My children. I'd thrown it all away in one idiotic moment and you are right, Agent Fall. I didn't stand a chance from the time Amanda walked into my office that day. She played me. Perfectly. Every step of the way. And I couldn't believe how angry that made me."

His voice rose. The hand holding the gun twitched and Stella saw his finger start to tighten. All her attention was focused on that finger. She had to delay him.

"Is that why you stabbed her so many times? Because you were angry?" she asked, thankful that her voice sounded calm. Visible panic would ignite his own fear and send him over the edge.

To her surprise, he shook his head.

"I needed to make sure she was dead. I couldn't bear the thought that she might somehow survive, and destroy me," he said quietly.

Stella felt shocked by the cold-bloodedness of his actions. She'd assumed it had been in anger and passion. He'd just proved her wrong.

"Don't you think you should put the gun down now?" she asked in a reasonable tone.

"No. I'm not going to do that. I am not a stupid man, Agent Fall," Oliver said to Stella. "You came here alone. Ever since you walked in, I've been thinking of how I could save myself if you suspected me. And this is the only scenario I can think of."

"What scenario?" Stella asked. She felt breathless now, lightheaded with fear. While she'd been trying to force a confession out of him, he'd been plotting his own course of action. No wonder he hadn't reacted as she'd expected him to.

"This is my plan. I didn't know you were arriving and in fact, you just walked in and started searching the house. I heard an intruder in the study, and now, I burst into the room and found you here. I will tell the police I shot you in a moment of terror when I saw you standing near the safe, which is in that very corner. All I saw was the knife in your hand."

"I don't have a knife in my hand," Stella pointed out. Her hands had started to shake. She was too far away to disarm him. She couldn't risk rushing him. Not when he'd already proved he had no inhibitions to killing.

"You will be holding a knife by the time the police find you," Oliver said calmly. "I'll make sure of it. I'll tell them you were a threat. I had no idea who you were and was under extreme stress at the time. And I think my actions will seem justified."

Stella felt as if the breath had been knocked out of her. He'd set up a trap and was about to shoot her. He was hell-bent on seeing his plan through and would not listen to logic or reason. His plan was flimsy. She didn't know if it would work or if he'd get away with it, but by that time she'd be dead.

Fear had gripped him again, she saw; the same fear that had caused him to stab Amanda time after time to make sure she would not live to speak against him.

If she could buy only a minute, it might be all she needed. She needed to derail him somehow. A desperate plan formed in her mind.

It was the only solution she could think of but it might just work for long enough.

She turned around so that she had her back to him, facing the polished bookshelf where the steely outline of the safe was visible behind the rows of books.

"Good luck with your defense shooting me in the back," Stella said, with as much confidence as she could summon up. "Let's see how the jury feels about that."

Behind her, Stella heard Oliver's angry hiss.

"Evidence speaks for itself. If my back's turned and you shoot me, and I die here, there's not a jury alive who won't convict you for the crime."

She could feel the exact spot on her back where she thought the bullet would hit. Despairing, she realized that he was going to shoot regardless. Her life felt as if it was hanging by a thread. Never had she felt so helpless.

She continued, speaking rapidly.

"You do know your wife was cheating on you?" she asked in a conversational tone. "That's why this all happened."

Oliver laughed. "No, she wasn't," he retorted, but Stella picked up a note of uncertainty that hadn't been there before.

"Why do you think she couldn't give us an alibi for the night in question? It's not because she thought she was going to be trapped or that she was waiting for legal advice. It's because she was out, cheating, while you were killing Amanda."

"And you say that why?" Now he sounded on edge, rattled, as if he'd been in full control of the situation but now it was slipping away.

"I say it because we got a confession from other members of the little clique. From Juliet and Eleanor. They both admitted that those friendly bridge get-togethers were not just playing cards. In fact, they weren't playing cards at all. They were daring each other to cheat, choosing people that they'd met innocently in their day-to-day activities so that the phone calls wouldn't be noticed," Stella said, unable to keep the cynicism out of her voice.

"You're lying," Oliver shouted. His voice was starting to crack. She heard the stamp of his foot and realized he'd taken an angry step toward her. She cringed inwardly, expecting to feel the deadly punch of a bullet in a back.

But then she realized what he'd done.

He'd stepped toward her. His anger was making him want to physically assault her.

Suddenly, Stella realized that her only chance was to use his weakness, and provoke him enough to derail his plan. She had to bait him into attacking her. It was the only way to bring him close enough that she could try and get the gun away from him.

Words could be weapons. They were the only ones she had now.

"Amanda got dared," Stella continued. "But Amanda didn't take it well. In fact, she refused the dare. She was angry with Cassidy for trying to coerce her into doing it. So she planned her own revenge, and decided to sleep with you." Stella allowed a teasing note to creep into her voice "Do you see where you came into this now? You were being used as part of Amada's secret payback."

"She was going to destroy me," he hissed.

"Oh, no, she wasn't. You got it wrong," Stella taunted him. "Amanda just wanted the satisfaction of knowing she did it. She really would have kept it a secret. Just like all the other names in her little black book. She wouldn't have told Cassidy, because that would have exposed her, too. She never wanted to see your wife or the other friends again. She never intended to destroy you. You destroyed yourself! What a pity you refused to believe her! If you had, everything would be fine, but now look where it's gotten you. First you were a cheater, and then you were a coward, and now you're a criminal. Loser!"

The angry yell behind her made her flinch. Oliver had cracked. Enraged, he rushed her.

He fired the gun as she spun around. He was ready, but so was she. He was right-handed, so she spun to the left, twisting out of the way and knocking his hand with her arm so that the bullet went wide.

He swore violently, and then they were in contact. Stella was fighting for her life. He was taller and far stronger and it felt as if the gun was welded to his hand. He grabbed her hair and tugged at it viciously and she screamed in agony. She kicked at his knee and stamped down on his shiny shoe, causing him to swear in pain.

The gun went off again, a deafening blast.

"Stop it!" Oliver yelled again. He grabbed her hair and bashed her head against the edge of the shelf. Stella felt lights explode behind her eyes. Dizziness made her disoriented and she felt her grip on his wrist start to slip. This might be the end. This could be all it took. He'd kill her and muddy up the evidence enough that the others could never get to the truth.

Inexorably, Stella watched the muzzle of the gun swing around toward her. But then, she managed to fight back. She remembered the pepper spray exercise. Even disoriented and half-blinded, there was a technique she'd used to wrestle the gun back from the agent who'd tried to grab it from her.

Stella lunged forward, locking her fingers onto his wrist, ready for the twist that would hopefully disarm him, even though she was still off balance and far weaker than she had been in the training exercise. This was her only chance. She had to try, even if he fought back. Digging her nails into his flesh, Stella wished for the last fragment of strength she didn't have.

Grab and twist, that was what Marc had told her over and over again during training, when her hands were shaking from weakness and when she knew she couldn't do it one more time but she had to, and had somehow forced herself to, because the alternative would be to fail.

And then Stella remembered the last time, the final test and the worst challenge of all, when she'd been blinded and in agony thanks to the agonizing blast of the pepper spray in her eyes.

She was going to do it. From deep inside, she managed to summon the reserves of strength she needed, and twisted with all her might.

She did it. The gun slipped from Oliver's grasp as he cried out in pain and despair. It clattered to the floor. As hard as she could, Stella shoved him out of the way with her shoulder while she dove down and grabbed it.

She jumped back, out of reach, pointing it at his chest.

"Do not move!" she yelled. "Stand where you are. Hands in the air! If you move, I will shoot!"

Horror filled Oliver's face as he slowly raised his arms.

Watching his final capitulation, Stella felt grateful beyond words that she'd survived the struggle. And then, approaching the door, she heard a clatter of running feet.

Relief filled her as Maxwell rushed into the room.

"FBI! You are under arrest!" he shouted to Oliver.

Finally, her backup had arrived.

*

Stella climbed out of the passenger seat at the police station, feeling a deep sense of relief that an evil person was safely in police custody. She knew Oliver would have killed again. He would have done whatever it took to keep his name clear and protect himself. His version of reality had been far removed from what was normal.

"Cassidy will probably get bail tomorrow—which Oliver won't—but she'll still be facing charges as a result of her behavior toward us at the spa," Maxwell explained as he got out of the driver's side. When he'd heard about Stella's bash to the head, he'd insisted on driving her unmarked there himself, for safety's sake. One of the other police was following in his car.

"Everything she's done will be exposed," Maxwell continued. "Likewise, Juliet and Eleanor. No more secrets. Their hobbies will be out in the open. I doubt anyone will forgive what they have done."

"Yes. They've ruined their lives," Stella agreed. "I think it's sad."

"Could have lived in comfortable bliss," Maxwell said. He glanced at Stella as they walked inside, and for the first time she thought he was maybe a little unsure about who she really was.

She hoped so. She had enough enemies waiting for her back at the academy without Maxwell adding to their numbers.

The police were busy processing Oliver's arrest, but as soon as Roth saw her, he left the group and hurried over to meet her at the door.

"I must congratulate you, Fall," he said. "You were like a bulldog on this case. You didn't give up. You kept pushing for every angle and every lead, even when it seemed to go nowhere. Your determination paid off. Now we have the right suspect arrested, instead of a frustrating case that would have made everyone involved look incompetent, and most probably gotten cold."

Taking a deep breath, Stella said what she needed to say.

"I only managed to do it because of everything I've learned since being here, and everything you've taught me. I feel like this has been the best experience of my life."

With a satisfied nod, Roth returned to the group of detectives, and Stella turned back to Maxwell, speaking in a quieter voice.

"I know you didn't want me on the case. I've been meaning to tell you that I'm not really who you think I am at all. I don't have connections. Only Clem, my university mentor, who happened to be at New Haven when the case was called in. He didn't try and push me onto it for no reason. Nobody was trying to give me an unfair advantage. And my recent background and the time in Greenwich is very different from where I came from."

"Yeah. Yeah, I sort of figured that out as we worked together," Maxwell said, sounding abashed. "I should have told you before that I'd changed my mind, and asked you more about it, but then things got crazy and there wasn't time."

"They did get crazy," Stella agreed with a smile. She felt relieved, and surprisingly pleased, that Maxwell had worked out she had gotten to where she was through merit, rather than any favoritism shown.

"Anyway. I wish you well," he said.

"I'll need it," Stella said ruefully, as her fears about the future rushed in to cloud her deep gratitude for having survived this case.

"Perhaps we'll bump into each other again one day," Maxwell said.

"Perhaps," Stella agreed, even though only she knew how unlikely this was.

"If we do, we grab another drink together. Okay? And this time, you talk about yourself. I'll be watching out for it. I got your number now, Stella Fall. Figuratively speaking at least," Maxwell said, with a surprisingly charismatic grin.

Now it was Stella's turn to blush. He'd realized that she'd deliberately turned the conversation away from herself. She found she liked Maxwell a lot more than she'd expected. He was very perceptive. And, when he smiled that way, she had to admit he was also easier on the eye than she'd realized. How strange was that?

"It's a deal," she promised him.

CHAPTER TWENTY NINE

At nine a.m. the next morning, Stella walked down the corridor that led to the director's office with terror boiling inside her. Marc had ordered her to report there as soon as she landed back at the academy. She'd spent the helicopter flight feeling if she was heading to her doom, and wishing that she could be somewhere else, anywhere else.

How could she have allowed herself to do something she would regret so badly? Why, oh why, had she been so irresponsibly hotheaded toward Carrie?

Talk about a life lesson learned too late, Stella thought sadly. How she wished things could have gone differently, and that she hadn't messed up. Especially now, after she'd been given the opportunity to work with the FBI on an actual case, and had a real taste of what the career was like.

Her dad would have been proud of what she'd done in the past two days. If only he was still around, so she could share her achievement with somebody who understood. He'd have applauded the way she'd fought for her life. He'd have thumped the table in appreciation when she explained the logical reasoning that had led her to the conclusion. Even though she'd only known him as a child, she could translate the way he'd respond to Stella the adult.

She could see, as if in vivid real life, how his face would light up. He'd get that shine in his eyes, that was more of a gleam than a spark, and which told her more clearly than words how his passion and commitment to his calling had shaped his life.

"Oh, Dad," Stella whispered, letting out a sigh.

Her father wasn't here for her now. Nobody was here, and she would have to face this trouble on her own.

Reaching the door, she saw the director's assistant was at his desk in the reception room. Unsmilingly he waved her straight through to the main office.

She paused outside the main door, gathering her courage. Then she tapped on the door.

"Come in," a voice called.

Stella had never been in the director's office before. The closest she'd come to it had been meeting Clem outside. It wasn't a place you went unless you were in trouble, or about to have a disciplinary hearing, or to be expelled.

All three awaited her inside.

She opened the door and stepped in, feeling numb with dread at what the next few minutes would bring.

The office was surprisingly plain. She'd imagined an oak-paneled sanctuary similar to the place where she had fought for her life with Oliver. But this room was minimalistically furnished, with a large, plain desk, a small, six-seater boardroom table, and a couple of big-screen TVs on the walls, which were also lined with framed photographs, certificates, awards, and other memorabilia.

The director himself sat behind his desk. Marc was at the boardroom table, tapping keys on his laptop. He glanced up when she entered. Her terrified gaze swiveled from his expressionless face to the director's impassive one.

As a new recruit, she'd been welcomed to the academy on her first day by the director, who had arrived in their classroom and spent a few minutes introducing himself, reminding them of the academy's ethos, and speaking to each of the trainees personally.

Stella had been impressed by his quiet, restrained manner which she could see understated the power that he held. He was a slim, spare man whose short-cropped, graying hair and fit physique spoke of a lifetime of training and discipline.

"Stella Fall," he said. He stood up.

"Yes, sir." She could hear the stress in her own voice.

"Unusual circumstances for us to be meeting again."

"They are, sir," she said.

Should she apologize? She had no idea what to do in this unprecedented situation. Her instincts were to fight, but she didn't know how to do it. How could she? She was one person, who had made a terrible mistake and was now facing the mechanisms of an established and powerful institution.

The director walked over to the boardroom table and took a seat next to Marc. He indicated the one opposite.

"Please join us."

Stella sat.

In desperation, she wondered how she should approach this. The course of this entire debacle had been decided the moment she'd lost control. There was no point in begging. The most she could do was to fully explain the mitigating circumstances, and the moments that had led up to this tipping point. And if that was unsuccessful, she was going to take her punishment with as much dignity as she could, and hope that she could salvage something, somehow, to take forward to another career.

Bitterly, she thought of how she would miss the adrenaline rush of being involved in an FBI-level investigation.

"So, let's go over the facts of the matter," the director said in a neutral voice. "Marc?"

Marc met her eyes. His gaze was like a laser beam.

"Trainee agent Carrie Potts laid an official complaint against you two days ago. Her account of events stated the following. She said that you deliberately punched her in the solar plexus while you were waiting at the start of the obstacle course. You then knocked her off her feet, which caused her to fall backward and badly sprain her left wrist. This in turn meant that she did not complete the final physical challenge."

Stella felt as if she was turned to stone. That wasn't what had happened! Not at all. She hadn't sprained her wrist. She'd landed squarely on her skinny butt, in the mud. And what was this about not completing the challenge because of the sprain? How had she even managed to start it if her wrist had been so badly injured?

She'd imagined that she would have to accept a truthful account. But an inaccurate one? That put a whole different spin on things. In that moment, Stella knew she would have to stand up for herself, no matter what.

"Ms. Potts said this was a deliberate action on your part to try to make sure she did not graduate. As it happens she passed the other tests so she will graduate regardless, but she is adamant that this was attempted sabotage."

Stella felt herself wilting under Marc's piercing gaze.

"So, what is your version of events?" he said.

Stella's mouth felt dry.

"It's different. That's not what happened. Yes, we were waiting at the start of the obstacle course, but she began baiting me. Sir, she's had issues with me ever since the start of the training program. There have been a few episodes between us that I never mentioned as I decided that it would be better to ignore them. Anyway, when she started taunting me I responded and she became angry. She was about to lunge at me. I decided that it would be better to quickly put her down, instead of having it turn into a damaging fight."

"So what did you do?"

"I punched her in the solar plexus. Then I knocked her off her feet using a maneuver that we were taught in our training sessions. She landed in the mud on her butt."

There was an odd noise from the director and Stella glanced at him. He looked poker-faced. Perhaps he'd just suppressed a cough, she decided, continuing with her account.

"I definitely didn't notice anything wrong with her wrist. At that point, you told my partner and me to start the course, so we went. During the round, I started to regret what I'd done. It had felt like the only solution at the time, but I started to realize that I had been too hotheaded. When Carrie finished her course, I planned to apologize to her. However, before I saw her again, I was called away by Thom, and ended up going to New Haven to help with the case."

Stella felt breathless as she finished her account. She'd been as truthful as she could, and hoped she hadn't ended up being overly honest. What would they think? Did they believe her? Did what she'd said even matter?

"Thank you for your version," Marc said.

Stella waited. What would happen now? It seemed Marc had more to say.

"There is little common ground between your accounts. But fortunately there were witnesses to the altercation between you. Four of your fellow trainees were there. So I interviewed them to find out what they had to say."

Now Stella's heart felt as if it was going a hundred miles an hour. Her mind went back to that terrible day, at the start of her training, when she'd realized the men resented her for her shooting prowess and that Carrie was the more popular of the two of them.

None of them would have seen that first move by Carrie. Stella had picked it up too fast.

She waited for her fate to be decided, not daring to glance at the director.

"One of your fellow trainees said he didn't see anything at all. He was tying his shoelace at the time," Marc said.

Stella blinked. Nobody had been adjusting their footwear! She was the only one who'd fixed a lace. They'd all been glued to the scene that had played out.

"Another said he didn't see what had happened because he'd been watching the pair ahead of him start the course," Marc continued.

Now Stella's heart was banging in her throat. What was happening? Why were they doing this?

"The third of the group said that he recalls you gave Carrie a friendly push after joking with her, but that he didn't remember her falling over although she might have stumbled on a tree root."

"I see," she said, feeling she should say something even though she didn't see at all. What was happening here?

"The fourth and final witness was the one who partnered with Carrie during her physical test. He didn't see any fight between you, but said that on the third obstacle, the tilting ladder, Carrie lost her grip when she was halfway up and fell, landing heavily on her wrist. He stopped to ask her if she was all right. When she said she wasn't, he told her that she should not try to complete the course but should walk straight back to the start and get medical attention for the fall."

Stella couldn't understand this. She felt like bursting into tears. The final witness had related the true account of how the injury occurred, still without mentioning the fight. He hadn't had to do that. None of them had. They'd all gone out of their way to ensure that Carrie's version didn't hold any water.

Up until that point, Stella had been sure that everyone in her team was on Carrie's side. Now, she realized that they had been at first. But during those long and challenging months, during the physical tests and the shooting practice and the awful pepper spray test—maybe they had come to think of Stella as a friend, too. As someone that they could trust and should protect. As one of them.

She couldn't believe that had happened. She had thought it never would.

"What about my version? I've been going through hell about it. I know what I did was wrong," she asked, her throat now all choked up. Her version was the only one that had admitted to guilt. The only one apart from Carrie's, as it happened.

"It's clear from the eyewitness accounts that the main injury must have occurred during the physical test. Our medic confirmed this and said that with such a bad sprain, it's unlikely Ms. Potts would have been able to do the previous obstacles at all, at any rate, not without significant pain. The take-home conclusion is that there are disparities in the accounts that contradict the original report's content. Given all of this, we will not be taking any further action. We regard whatever happened as a minor incident that should have been personally resolved and not escalated."

Stella stared at Marc in shock, unable to believe this incredible outcome.

"As far as your version goes, Ms. Fall, you have proved to us that you've punished yourself enough. Let this be a warning to you. Do not ever raise your hand to a fellow FBI agent again. No matter the circumstances or the provocation."

"I promise I will learn from this, sir," she said, her mouth dry.

And then his words sunk in. He'd said a fellow FBI agent. Did that mean they would allow her to graduate?

"Good. See you at the ceremony. I have nothing further to add," Marc said.

The director cleared his throat. "I do," he said.

Stella hesitated, feeling her fragile confidence shatter. She'd just been told she could graduate, but now she worried that trouble would come crashing down on her shoulders again.

"I would like to commend you on your conduct during this recent investigation. This was a big challenge for a trainee."

How had he known about it? Stella wondered, as she turned to him in surprise. His next words explained.

"Agent Roth called me an hour ago, while he was driving. He apologized for not having had time to compile a report, but he wanted me to know, before you landed, that you were a huge asset to the team. Your commitment to the case and your insight and quick thinking were pivotal in solving it. He also emphasized you had shown great courage, tenacity, and perceptiveness, as well as extreme calmness under pressure. Well done, Agent Fall."

Now Stella could hardly hold back the tears. The director seemed to be swimming in an underwater lake as she offered him a heartfelt "Thank you, sir. Thank you so much. I'm so glad I was able to assist, and the experience was invaluable. I hope I will be able to learn from it going forward."

"Thank you, Agent Fall," the director said again.

Stella stumbled out of the office, unable to process what had just happened.

It had all turned out okay. She was still an agent. She would graduate. And the director himself had commended her!

Being able to dream about a future, a real future in the FBI, felt like one of the happiest moments she'd ever had.

CHAPTER THIRTY

Four days later, Stella couldn't believe she had reached this point. She was standing at the foot of the large stage, waiting for her name to be called so that she could receive her personal handshake, as well as her official FBI badge, from the academy director.

It was a massive ceremony. Stella had never dreamed it would be so high powered. There were hundreds of people in attendance, including the friends and family of the new agents, as well as local government representatives, senators, and police chiefs.

To commemorate the occasion. Carrie had brought along her mother, who was tall, lean, and haughty, just like her. Brian, her fellow trainee, had his wife and two children at the event and Stella saw his face light up as he walked on stage and stared out at them.

"Stella Fall," Marc called her name.

She climbed the stairs and walked across the stage to the smiling director. Proudly, she raised her right hand and repeated the oath after him. He handed her the badge and she stared down at it, admiring how the gold gleamed. Her badge! At last, she was a full-fledged agent. Glancing down at the waiting guests, she felt grateful that Clem, who had gotten her into the program, was here watching her graduate. He was like a father to her. She knew he thought of her as his own daughter. She couldn't be happier that he was there, and that she had someone special in attendance at this time.

Although, who else was there, waving at her?

Stella felt curious as she saw Roth at the back of the hall. He grinned appreciatively and applauded as she turned to the director for a final handshake.

Roth? Why was he here? She didn't think he was connected to any of the graduates. And he didn't know her well, either. Much as she'd like to compliment herself that she'd been such an asset that he'd arrived to watch her graduate, Stella didn't buy it. Perhaps he was going to debrief the new trainees on the recent case, she reasoned.

In another minute, the remaining agents had received their diplomas.

"We now have our special awards to give out, for top performance in all the categories—physical fitness, firearms, and academic," the director said, before reading out the winners' names.

Stella knew she would not be achieving any of them. She was proud of the scores she'd managed in every category but she was not top of the class in any of them. She was highest in the academic category but Brian had just beaten her final results and she couldn't be more pleased for him. As he went up to receive his trophy, she clapped so hard her hands hurt.

Then the director spoke again.

"Our final award is the Director's Leadership Award. This is for the candidate who has excelled in all fields and who has shown exceptional ability throughout their training. The award is decided upon by the director and staff, and the nomination is then confirmed by the nominee's peers. We are delighted that for the very first time, this award has been earned by one of our female graduates." He paused. Out of the corner of her eye, Stella saw Carrie sit straighter.

"Stella Fall, congratulations!"

A round of applause thundered around the hall.

Her? How was this possible? Feeling as if she might be dreaming, Stella hurried out of line and climbed the stairs again to receive her award. The proud gleam in the director's eyes made her feel ten feet tall.

She returned to her seat, clutching the trophy, feeling proud and tearful and filled with gratitude as the director closed the ceremony and thanked the audience, the graduates, and the VIP guests for attending.

Then, leaping up from her seat, Stella hurried over to greet Clem.

"I'm so glad you could make it," she said.

"I'm very proud to be here." Clem smiled. "It's not often you get to watch a family member graduating. Or the closest thing to family, anyway. And the director's award is a huge honor."

He squeezed her arm affectionately. Clem wasn't a big one for hugs.

"Have you heard where you've been assigned yet?" he asked her.

"No, not yet. Everyone else has been assigned, but not me. I was expecting to hear by yesterday," Stella said, feeling worried as she thought about the delay. Knowing where she'd be working was such a big step. Her whole career would be shaped by the first field office where she was assigned, and where she would then spend a probationary period as a new agent.

She hadn't named any preferences or listed any chosen areas where she would prefer to work when she'd filled in the form. For a while she'd wondered if she could ask not to be assigned anywhere in Kansas, but she'd decided against it. She needed to go where she would make a difference. If that proved to be Kansas then so be it; she'd endure her home state, with all its bad associations, somehow.

Even Carrie had come out of the office looking smug, after receiving her briefing. Of course, Stella hadn't spoken to her and had no idea where she'd be heading.

"I wouldn't be concerned about the delay," Clem said, and Stella thought he looked secretive now, as if he knew something she didn't.

At that moment, someone tapped her shoulder. She turned, and there was Roth.

"Congratulations on graduating, Agent Fall. And well done on earning the director's award. What an honor," he said, and she had never been more proud to be greeted with her new official title. Praise from this senior agent was high praise indeed.

"Thank you so much. It's great to see you," she said. She stopped there, knowing there was a question in her words.

"I came here because I wanted to speak to you personally," Roth said.

To speak to her? Stella felt completely taken aback.

Roth moved a few steps away to a quiet corner of the room.

"I want to offer you a job. You've already been assigned elsewhere, but I asked the director if I could make my offer to you first. I need an additional team member. You have skills that we need in our area, and that we don't currently have among our personnel. I like working with you and feel you have great potential. If you accept, you'll be working under me, in the New Haven office, investigating violent crimes and other federal crimes."

Roth wanted her? In New Haven?

Stella couldn't help having mixed feelings about the area where she'd be working, as she considered this otherwise amazing offer.

She'd left Connecticut originally after her fiancé's murder and everything that had followed, never thinking she'd be back there again. Then Clem had landed her there a second time. It was never a place she'd felt she belonged. There were so many traumatic memories associated with it.

But yet, she was used to it now. In a weird way, she felt she understood the place, even if it was definitely a love-hate relationship.

And she'd grown to respect Roth immensely. Though prickly and terse, he'd taught her a huge amount. She would gain the most incredible experience working with him.

Perhaps she'd even be able to go for that beer with Maxwell, Stella suddenly thought, wondering if he'd be happy to see her there or would resent her presence all over again.

Of course, she longed to know where she had been assigned before this offer overrode the posting, but she couldn't ask. This was a yes-no question and she needed to give the answer immediately.

Stella knew that for the sake of her career, and also for what she instinctively wanted, this was the right decision for her.

"I accept. I'm thrilled that you want me on your team. I can't imagine a better place to work, Roth," she said.

"That's excellent." She thought from the way he tried to suppress his smile, that he was even more pleased than he was letting on. "We'd like you to start in ten days. That will give you enough time to move, get settled, find a place. My office will help you with that, and sort you out for the first month. I know the area and can also give you some recommendations."

"Thank you so much," Stella said.

Roth had impressed her all over again with his immediate concern that she was able to settle in comfortably. It was a kindness and consideration that she appreciated. At any rate it showed there was a warm heart under that sometimes terse exterior.

"Just make sure you listen to me, right?" he said, now allowing a wide grin to warm his face.

Stella decided to risk a little humor in return.

"I promise I will, sir," she retorted.

Roth guffawed.

"We look forward to having you with us. Make no mistake, it's not easy. Especially in this neighborhood. We all have to be at the top of our game, all the time, and there's zero room for error. Not with everyone and his lawyer watching us. Now, much as it hurts me to do this, I'd better go say a humble thank-you to Clem for twisting my arm to include you in the Logan case," he said.

With a final, approving nod, he turned and strode away.

CHAPTER THIRTY ONE

Stella couldn't believe her luck. She'd graduated from the FBI Academy and had won the Director's Award. In another week, she'd be starting her dream job at the office in New Haven, taking the first step in a career she'd always longed to follow.

And, best of all, in the meantime, she was spending some quality time with her friend in New Jersey.

She grinned at Rebecca as they headed toward the house, after completing a brisk walk around the nearby park. A brisk walk was Rebecca's concession to physical exercise. As she'd frequently told Stella, she loved to walk, she loved to hike, but under no circumstances was she prepared to run.

"Not even if something is chasing me," she joked as they approached the front door. "I'll rather stand my ground and fight it off!"

Stella laughed—rather breathlessly, because even though Rebecca claimed to be anti-running, she set a serious pace at a walk. Stella was more than ready for the dinner at the local pizza restaurant she was going to treat Rebecca and Marco to, as a celebration for getting the job and a thank-you for all they had done.

"When is Marco getting home?" she asked Rebecca, seeing her friend's face light up at her husband's name.

"He'll be back by seven. So we can book the table for seven-thirty."

"Let me pour us some water." Stella headed through to the kitchen, filled two glasses, and slumped down on a chair, feeling a sense of well-being. "It's so great to relax after these past few days."

"I'm so thrilled you solved the case. That's a huge feather in your cap. I must say, the details were chilling," Rebecca agreed.

"They were. I felt sorry for Amanda in the end. It's as if her past came back to haunt her. She tried to be a better person after her move, but then the dare and the threats triggered her and she went all the way back again."

"Yes. I also felt conflicted hearing that. But perhaps she'd have ended up repeating her mistakes in any case."

"Well, she got what she wanted in terms of bringing down the others. She got more than she could have dreamed of in terms of payback. None of them will be doing that again," Stella said solemnly.

"True." Rebecca put down her empty glass. "Right. What shall we do now? We have an hour before we need to get ready."

"I need to go through the rest of my stuff," Stella decided.

That was a job she'd been putting off since her arrival two days ago, but it had to be done. Rebecca had kindly stored a few of Stella's boxes while she'd been at Quantico. Now, she needed to organize the contents before her big move to New Haven, where Roth had already chosen her a stunning, petite apartment. He'd sent Stella photos of the building and the neighborhood and she couldn't believe her luck. It overlooked a park, and being on the fifth floor and east facing, also had a faraway view of the sea.

It's only drawback, if you could call it that, was that it was a compact, one-bed bachelor pad, so Stella didn't want to take unnecessary junk with her. And she had unnecessary junk. These four large boxes up in Rebecca's attic had stood untouched in her apartment during her student days. She knew they contained stuff from her home and childhood. She had shied away from looking inside, feeling reluctant to have memories of her father intrude. Now it was time to open up, sort through, and clear out. She didn't want to take any baggage with her to her new place.

"That's not a job to do alone." Rebecca picked up immediately that Stella felt reluctant to face her old papers and possessions. "I'll come up and help you. Let's see if we can break the back of this horrible job. Maybe even finish it. I'll bring some trash bags up as I'm sure you'll be throwing a lot of it away," she said encouragingly.

They headed up the staircase to the second floor, and then crept up the even steeper stairs that led to the attic. Here, in the surprisingly spacious top floor, Stella's boxes had been stashed in a corner.

She dragged the first one out, ready for the memories that would overpower her as she opened it. Even the smell of home might still be lingering in papers and among folds of fabric, she realized. She didn't want it. It made her feel sick. How she wished she could just erase her first sixteen years of life and never think about it again.

Rebecca rummaged in a drawer, found a pair of scissors, and cut open the old, dusty tape that was tightly wrapped around the box. In fact, Stella thought, the tape was all that was stopping the ancient cardboard from collapsing.

"These are school books. Why did I pack school books?" Stella asked in bewilderment as she removed the top layer. "Oh, I remember!"

"Why?" Rebecca quizzed.

"The poetry. There are some amazing poetry collections in these books, and I particularly loved our final year's plays. *Antigone. Hamlet.* True classics with so much insight."

"You can see why you headed straight into psychology." Rebecca smiled.

Stella felt better as she stacked the books into the keepers pile. There was nothing bad in this box. Nothing that would anger her ghosts, as she wryly thought, and risk giving her nightmares for weeks ahead.

Or so she thought, until the next layer came into view.

"Oh, no." Emotions surged inside her as she looked at the roughly carved ornaments. "My dad made these for me in his workshop. That used to be my refuge, where I'd hide from the world."

Rebecca's sympathetic nod told her that she knew it hadn't been the world that Stella had been hiding from, but rather from Rhonda Fall's constant, vicious abuse.

"What are these?" Rebecca asked, distracting Stella from her examination of the toys that held so many memories.

"Those? I don't know. They look like letters. What are they doing in the box?"

Stella thought back to when she'd packed it. The memories were shrouded in the past. She guessed she'd gone through the drawers in the house and simply upended the contents into a box if they looked relevant.

"Oh," she said, feeling as if a knife had pierced her heart. "It's a letter from my dad. To my mother. He hardly ever wrote them. The ones I've seen were all very old, before I was born. Before things soured between them," she said sadly.

She opened the letter.

It was very short. After opening with a formal greeting, the neatly penned words in the second paragraph immediately caught her eye.

"Please, when she's ready, tell Stella. Perhaps she can forgive me one day."

Tell Stella? What should she have been told? Had her father had a secret life? This had clearly been written after she was around, so it was not an older letter.

Feeling suddenly sick with dread, Stella reread the letter, but it offered no further clues.

Until she saw the postmark on the envelope.

Then she let out an audible gasp, causing Rebecca, who was sorting through more English books, to look up in concern.

"Rebecca. Look here. Just look. I don't believe this!" Stella said. Her voice sounded high and shrill. She felt as if she'd been dragged into a nightmarish alternate reality. How could this possibly be true?

"What is it?" her friend asked, now sounding panicked. "Stella, it's okay. Whatever it is, it's from long ago. We can handle it. We'll get past it."

"No. No, we won't. Look here. Look at this postmark!" With shaking hands, now hyperventilating from stress, Stella pointed to it.

"It's two months after my dad disappeared. Two months!"

"No!" Rebecca said, looking shocked. Her face had turned ashen. "Are you sure you're right? You're not confusing the dates? The post office couldn't have made an error?"

"It can't be a mistake. It must be true. But now it feels like my whole life since then has been a lie!" Stella felt rage sharpen inside her, as vicious as a blade.

"I can't believe it," Rebecca whispered.

"I always wondered how he could have disappeared without a trace and why his body was never found. But this tells me he went away. He asked my mother to explain it to me, and she never did. That's even worse! Where did he go? Did he change his name? How do I find him, and is he still even alive now?" Stella stared at her friend in consternation. "Why, why, why did he do such a thing, and why did she not tell me, like he asked her?"

Rebecca shrugged helplessly, looking as traumatized as Stella felt.

"I've no idea. But you need to find out."

Stella's hatred toward her mother now felt more powerful than any she'd had in the past. How could she have blatantly lied that she had no idea where Stella's father was, or what had happened? How could she have kept this information from her own daughter, cruelly and deliberately, for so many years?

This wasn't a job for a phone call, Stella resolved.

"I'm going to have to go back home."

She was going to have to return to the place she hated most in the world. And she was going to have to confront her abusive, domineering mother. She needed to look her in the eye and find out, at last, the real truth about her father.

NOW AVAILABLE FOR PRE-ORDER!

HIS OTHER SECRET
(A Stella Fall Psychological Suspense Thriller—Book 3)

HIS OTHER SECRET is book #3 in a new psychological suspense series by debut author Ava Strong, which begins with HIS OTHER WIFE (Book #1).

When a popular local fitness instructor is found murdered in a wealthy suburb, FBI Special Agent Stella Fall is dispatched to an ultra-exclusive Connecticut coastal town. She soon discovers the town is rife with secrets, and pulls back the veil on a circle of cheating wives who had turned their cycling class into a cult. In this insular, exclusive yacht club community, no one is talking; everything seems perfect. But behind the perfect facades, everything, Stella soon learns, is rotten to its core. This gossipy and back-biting town is hiding sinister secrets and vendettas, and Stella, recognizing it from her own past, is determined to use her brilliant mind to probe their psychology and out the killer.

Meanwhile, Stella can't help but feel a connection to her new FBI partner. But when she is summoned to unexpectedly confront her demeaning, narcissistic mother about the secrets of her past, old wounds are stirred up in Stella's fragile psyche, and the shocking revelations of her childhood may just derail her for good.

A fast-paced psychological suspense thriller with unforgettable characters and heart-pounding suspense, HIS OTHER SECRET is book #3 in a riveting new series that will leave you turning pages late into the night.

Future books in the series will be available soon.

Ava Strong

Debut author Ava Strong is author of the REMI LAURENT mystery series, comprising three books (and counting); of the ILSE BECK mystery series, comprising four books (and counting); and of the STELLA FALL psychological suspense thriller series, comprising three books (and counting).

An avid reader and lifelong fan of the mystery and thriller genres, Ava loves to hear from you, so please feel free to visit www.avastrongauthor.com to learn more and stay in touch.

BOOKS BY AVA STRONG

REMI LAURENT FBI SUSPENSE THRILLER
THE DEATH CODE (Book #1)
THE MURDER CODE (Book #2)
THE MALICE CODE (Book #3)

ILSE BECK FBI SUSPENSE THRILLER
NOT LIKE US (Book #1)
NOT LIKE HE SEEMED (Book #2)
NOT LIKE YESTERDAY (Book #3)
NOT LIKE THIS (Book #4)

STELLA FALL PSYCHOLOGICAL SUSPENSE THRILLER
HIS OTHER WIFE (Book #1)
HIS OTHER LIE (Book #2)
HIS OTHER SECRET (Book #3)

www.ingramcontent.com/pod-product-compliance
Lightning Source LLC
Chambersburg PA
CBHW030616310726
48979CB00003B/738

* 9 7 8 1 0 9 4 3 9 2 6 6 0 *